SCIENCE FICTION ANTHOLOGY

Associated ASIN B09QY67FXT

Copyright 2022 Charles J Marino

All Rights Reserved. No part of this book may be reproduced or used in any manner without the permission of the copyright owner except for brief quotations in a book review.

Library of Congress Control Number: 2022911710

Published individually by the author between 2013 - 2021 This edition contains revisions and additions.

"Mutant Escape" ISBN 9781005324681
'Tattoo World" ISBN 9781370314263 and 9781370345939
"Seed Ship" ISBN: 9780463214718
"A Little More Oxygen" ISBN: 9780463941157
"The Arvidson Legacy" ISBN 9780463026816
"Veil of Dreams" ISBN 9780463961957
"Demeter Unbound" including 'The Sweet Earth' ISBN 9781370070145 and 9781370279043

cover: courtesy of NASA – space debris orbiting Earth

Charles J Marino, Erudite First Editions
www.linkedin.com/in/charles-j-marino-publishing

1

CHARLIE MARINO

Dedication:

*To my pseudo-sister Gracie, without whom this volume
would never have seen the light of day.
Blame her!*

CONTENTS

Author Preface

Mutant Escape

Tattoo World

Seed Ship

A Little More Oxygen

The Arvidson Legacy

Veil of Dreams

Demeter Unbound

AUTHOR PREFACE

Each of these stories presents what I as a scientist consider to, unfortunately, be likely extensions of the current state of human affairs. The exception is 'A Little More Oxygen' which delves into the distant pre-history of our species.

When combined with human nature, unchanged for millennia, our present technology invites far more opportunities for disaster than utopia. There will always be those among us who are both technologically adept and have sufficient ethical fiber to resist the easy paths to power or gratification. Yet I have found them to be uniformly outnumbered.

It is said that no one is a villain in their own mind, too true, and few are villains all the time. However, given the natural impulse for intelligent action to be reduced as crowd numbers grow, and couple it with media linkage and how few are those among us who understand the tech behind throwing a light switch – no less atomic bombs, spacecraft, and the stock market – the few will continue to rule the many and be mostly unseen doing it. Unseen is untouched and empathy dies.

The tech will only grow. It has extended life expectancy from the 30s to the 80s. Yet I fear it will also exacerbate all the natural aspects of man noted above until even the capable and well-meaning, few as they are, become helpless before it.

These stories may be taken as entertainment, as warnings to begin preparations by those who can, or as predictions of the inevitable historic repetition. Only now, in the 21st century, errors made by creatures hurling rocks and spears will no longer be confined to the arm strength of a single human.

Beware.

CJM - Sol-3, Orion arm, Milky Way, Virgo Supercluster

MUTANT ESCAPE

One day in the spring of the northern hemisphere an object arrived. Or almost arrived, as it only first appeared once in orbit around the moon. The odds of a natural object like a comet or asteroid falling into the gravity well between Earth and Moon with just the right velocity and at just the right angle to achieve orbit were too large to be credible. Yet the people of Earth detected no electromagnetic nor heat signature. No chemical engine exhaust.

The debris orbiting Earth from its native technological species now numbered 37,000 pieces of "space junk," being tracked by the US Department of Defense's global Space Surveillance Network (SSN) sensors. Earth even had experience with an old rocket from a Surveyor-2 moon landing mission getting nabbed by Earth's gravity and becoming a miniature moon 54 years after it was discarded.

This wasn't one of ours.

Once a controlled vessel of some type, and just as clearly beyond Earth capabilities, it appeared from images taken by the international moon base at Ceres crater to be just another meteor. Heavy scarring on its rocky ovoid surface, but still too smoothly curved to be thought anything but a ship, lined with natural rock on its exterior. Or perhaps was once an asteroid tunneled out for natural shielding.

Completely unknown was whether benign or heralding invasion. The only thing known for certain was its mass and that it appeared to be dead in orbit, sliding into moon orbit from a gentle ballistic trajectory and unaltered since.

Of course, none of this was made public. At the first indications, all transmissions from a moon base and the three Earth space stations were delayed and edited by controlling governments. All felt we must impose complete secrecy to avoid panic.

NASA employed a pair of large transport ships from a private contractor, bringing supplies to the moon base during construction, and ferrying back valuable ores to help pay for the missions. The ores were catapulted into orbit with huge machines resembling a combination of trebuchet and mass driver. It was therefore given to the United States by the international community to redirect its next pair of rockets, one already on the pad and both near their launch windows, to intercept the object in moon orbit and if possible, board it. The President, of course, being a paranoid bully and facing the end of his second and final presidential term, saw an opportunity in fear, as always. He in turn assigned control and coordination to his Vice President, who in turn looked to loyal NSA/ICE extremists as secrecy and border penetration experts. This was a viable foreign threat if anything was. A science team from various SETI organizations and exoplanet research groups was rapidly cobbled together and soon deployed for the mission of their lives.

The lead was a three initial agency director tasked personally by the Vice President. He was in a foul mood. An alien arrival was not part of his plan to be the next Vice President, and perhaps more.

"It's bad enough we have to deal with these genetic freaks appearing here and there. The 'next evolutionary step in man' my pink Homo Sapien ass. We must force politicians to begin instituting DNA tests on newborns to find them as they appear. By the time they're 11 or 12, the few we knew of have all disappeared and who knows what they are up to. I for one will not let them replace us. If all I'm allowed to do so far is study and tag and monitor them, so be it. But that never stopped men of character from ultimately killing niggers or Jews or whomever they needed to protect their own."

Growing in vehemence he continued.

"In the early 20th century, our own country was wise enough to have a eugenics program to sterilize mongrels, or the retarded, or those with severe inheritable diseases. After almost 20 years of culling, the bleeding hearts shut them down with a great outcry, but their work helped make us strong, making us one of only three superpowers in the 21st century. Others were doing the same. If we were still doing it, just think how advanced and healthy Americans would be? But these dirty mutants! Yes, that's how we have to categorize them. They're not healthy, all appearances to the contrary. We must destroy them before they can breed another generation of filthy mutants. We'll blame something. Another Chinese virus attack or a Russian genetic experiment gone wrong. A chemical company or pharma giant ripe for a fall."

Then slowly, "No mention of Darwin or supermen on anyone's lips at this agency or I'll have their ass. These are just *dangerous aberrations*."

He appeared calmer suddenly, something his staff had grown used to but which was still startling to visitors.

"The political climate will turn the first time mutants do something overt, and they will. I can guarantee it. The VP will love it when I give him a video of them burning an inverted cross in front of a church, like when we made it look like black protesters burnt their own neighborhoods during the Covid 19 summer riots. When our political shift comes, and it always does, we'll be ready to act across the board. The VP is a rabid evangelist, and will easily carry the electoral vote next year. He sees sin everywhere, and these mutants are made to order. I'll deliver and when he wins the Presidency he'll deliver the VP seat to me!"

He smiled a shark smile. "Now tell me what we have on this dead alien ship. Just circling the moon, is it? Get me the boarding party team leader. First, get his superior."

Less than ten days later, a co-opted NASA transport was speeding its way into moon orbit. Contact in less than 2 days. On matching velocities, an external hull survey found several of what might be hatches of varying size. There were even smooth glass-like colored sections taken for instrument lights or control panels. Nothing appeared powered. The decision to have a welder robot cut thru one of the smaller hatches alarmed scientists who wanted months if not years of study before such a move, but they were easily ignored as men without power often are.

The breach proved benign. On opening, the only action was by an astronaut tasked with using a pumping apparatus to try and capture the internal atmosphere as it escaped the breach. Aside from welding and cutting particulates and gasses, on later testing it would prove remarkably similar to that on Earth. The science crew overrode military paranoia that it possibly came from Earth, saying instead likely this was a key reason for aliens coming here of all the choices in our system.

As an oval, the volume enclosed by the shell was enormous. Easily the length of the aging ISS, it held several floors of cargo in a seashell spiral arrangement from the outermost level down to a central core housing what proved to be a control room. As they made their way inside, one of the commandos commented that it resembled a spherical parking garage, where each level was reached by a huge ramp from the level above, or in this case, from the outside in. In a rare point of agreement, one of the scientists had to agree with this accurate assessment. "Yes. Like an Allonautilus Perforatus, a common seashell." This earned him a condescending glance from the nearest commandos.

The human International Space Station was far different. Cobbled together using small cylindrical sections and several solar panel wings. The largest manmade object in orbit, it was hoped by many of these same scientists that a replacement would be in orbit by now. Radiation embrittlement had taken its toll, plus we had learned a lot from its years in high Earth orbit. Replacement proved not to be in the cards as several nations launched their own stations in a period where the lack of international cooperation doomed another ISS.

Once aboard the dark alien vessel was seen evidence of a very advanced effort to transport life forms from the alien homeworld to another location. That was its only cargo. The scientists would not commit that Earth was, in fact, the original destination. Seed canisters loaded into what appeared as simple mortars for atmospheric drops, plus easily recognizable alien embryos and fetus samples in transparent containers filled racks everywhere aboard. Simple life forms all. Several small craft thought to be planetary glide shuttles were found on the outermost layer, but the commandos related strict orders that no breach of them would be attempted just yet.

A control room at the core was breached, with no damaging effects noted. There were not even organic pilots, rotting in their chairs. But there were several somethings which could pass for chairs. And no power at all even on what was recognized as control panels and flight instrumentation.

It was an automated ship, which had run its course. Designed with the option for manual flight, this automated 'panspermia' mission - as it would become known - could keep scientists in their glory for decades as they tried to decipher a language not of this Earth, unknown propulsion systems, and debate whether interstellar radiation levels had finally taken their toll to end their mission. One theory had imminent systems failure forcing the ship into an orbit around the nearest body. The only thing for certain was that not even plant seeds from another world had survived. Perhaps the DNA, if they had DNA or RNA, could still be analyzed even after interstellar radiation had done its worst.

The international community complained and would continue to complain when the United States unilaterally claimed the ship and towed it back using both heavy NASA transports. Russia claiming Venus in 2020, and again three years later had soured the political mood. The derelict ship would remain in orbit adjacent to the American space station and be researched there, 'until a safe way was found to land it'. While complaints were loud and numerous, none were effective. The ambitious director now closest to the ear of the Vice President laughed in a way that frightened even his personal staff.

It was no more than several months later that a second object arrived. It did not orbit the moon on arrival but was coming straight for the Earth. Speculation was that before dying the first ship had signaled back that we had been found with an atmosphere similar to their own and gave directions.

Seeming to be more advanced, it was detected above the asteroid belt, then using Mars, slung in towards Venus, the sun itself in turn, slung out again and came right for Earth, establishing itself in geosynchronous orbit alongside the original ship. There the ship simply stopped.

"We have to go thru this all over again, but with more caution; this one might carry life." So thought the agency director who preferred to get back to the mutant problem that provided so much pleasure and power in squashing. The natural mutations of homo sapiens were appearing more frequently now, a fact which was not known by the general public. The public must remain unaware of this new distraction until a use could be made of the announcement. His use.

The panspermia team, as they had come to be known, had their difficulties operating in high secrecy and orbiting with the military leaning over their shoulders. Theirs, though, was less concerned with power than knowledge. Ship actions achieving orbit and the lack of radio signals indicated it too was a robotic ship on autopilot.

"This one came in at several times the velocity of the first! Relativistic. In interstellar space, it might have hit 25% the speed of light. It wasn't enough to use the planets to slow its arrival. This ship had to use the sun itself!"

"We can back calculate. Tell how far away it came from, but not an accurate direction beyond our asteroid belt. Perhaps the distance will be enough to tell which solar system of origin."

"How do you mean?"

"We don't know where the first ship came from, only a single data point, but can assume the same point of origin for both. In retrospect, we know that the first object was seen but not recognized traversing the asteroid belt a year before we found it in moon orbit. We estimated its speed from that combination."

The primary investigative team was in residence on the American station, while a rotating core of staff at NASA stood by in support until their turn came in orbit. With frenzied calculations written on a weightless clipboard, several others on the team gathered around the two brightest among them as they realized a new piece of knowledge was falling into place.

"Now compare the distance traveled for the second object coming at much higher speeds with an ungodly powerful engine. Plot both tracks backward until they intersect. Where they overlap, that must be the distance to point of origin. And gives us how far apart in time were the launchings. Just not an accurate direction."

Astounding. A mere century in time appears to have separated the launchings, yet that span was almost overcome as the superior second ship almost caught up. They may very well have assumed this last ship would overtake the first or arrive as it did shortly after. With improved engines, it should also have a better payload. More tech for preservation on the way here. Less time in the radiation of interstellar space. Even genetic modifications to the life forms sent to better survive the trip or - gulp - land when it got here. A hundred years of improvement in Earth tech of late had been a lot of tech. From 1860 horse buggies to 1960 space travel. Surely these aliens were not standing still all that time either.

The investigation crew was disappointed when at the calculated distance, no stars with planets in a habitable zone were known. They were back to square one on identifying the exact source. The still indecipherable records and instrument labels found aboard the first ship were no help either. At least for most of them. And most did not realize the flaw in the distance calculations...

***

In a warehouse not far from the NASA launch facility, a number of individuals in various scientific and business disciplines had gathered. The leader of this group was a tall slender young man, yet with an authority of command about him. In a room of high achievers, he easily held the floor.

"Only a pair of us got onto the research team for the first panspermia ship, but none of the astronauts sent to intercept and board were one of us. We must make certain that is not the case this time. This second ship still has powered engines."

These scientists soon found their discussion darkening over a risky new idea forming as they spoke. They already had a pair of their own aboard the American Orbital Station as part of the scientific team, likely impressing the bright but genetically slower Homo Sapien scientists. Up to three more individuals were on the ground team, scheduled to join them with their expertise in areas of metallurgy and linguistics. It was agreed that full use must be made of this penetration. With the international situation decaying, security screening for new staff would only increase.

The tall young man addressed them all. He put the proposition flatly before them. "Can we co-opt this ship and leave? Get on the initial boarding party, and at least one of us, take control already knowing their language and control systems. Land, pick us up, and get away from this bloody planet? We've already learned much of the language and control systems from the first derelict, and the normals have not. If we can extrapolate to this ship - I know it's a hundred years more advanced - what chance do we have of boarding it and trying for the Barnard-b planet?"

It was already agreed that a direction opposite the direction of the ships' origin seemed best, since if there were any viable planet the way they came it would have stopped there. So 180 degrees pointed to the Barnard system at only 6 lightyears off. In academic studies, it was one of the best candidates for a colonization effort. A way to escape the primitives. But technology to get there seemed another half a century away or more until these alien ships arrived. Fortunate, if only they could take advantage of the luck.

"We've better chances than the Sapiens, especially if we misdirect their research. So far they are clueless. Our people have put nothing on language in writing, relying on memory. Unless given the equivalent of a Rosetta stone to work with, I doubt they will crack it soon, especially with our people misdirecting them. Only we can read their manuals."

"For practicality of the voyage, a ship like this at 25% light speed could make the trip in 24 years, more like 27 with acceleration here and deceleration time there. We aren't even close to achieving these engines here, but the rest we have: incubators, hibernation units used for the Mars mission two years ago, 3d printers used to build the moon base, clone banks, all that... In less than 30 years, we'd be in the Barnard system. Slow down, scan, and put us in orbit above the best candidate planet or moon. We'll use the NASA robonauts to read scans and direct the ship to the right planet." The original robonauts were all remote controlled, but a big push had come during the Mars missions since radio signal time delay made AI autonomy critical. Robonauts were now the most autonomous machines on Earth outside military attack drones.

"Once in orbit robonauts wake us and begin landing protocols."

"If none at Barnard are viable, have the ship programmed to head out again, to Ross-128, then perhaps Luyten until we get one." Being the first such effort from Earth, the probabilities were incalculable. Anything adverse at the far end could doom the expedition.

"The way things are going here we must try. Once the Homo Sapiens found out about us, it was over. It is a race of dominance over them or extinction for us, and we don't have the numbers. We shall not be able to hide in plain sight much longer. They'll just keep getting better at DNA tests of newborns to identify us and retinal scans of adults to cull us out of their herd. We're screwed here. The politicians who initially found it publicly unacceptable to talk of killing healthy looking babies in their cribs are finding public acceptance for culling to be increasing. Someone in power is actively working against us."

"Our young are maturing so much faster than the normals that long before graduating elementary school, our kind soar past their own 'normal' children, even when born into normal families. The pressure is coming not just from the religious fanatics, protecting 'god's own' chosen people. Some normals have already euthanized children of kindergarten age without government sanction."

"Such is their fear of us."

"Let's hope we don't have to leapfrog as far as Kepler-1649c, circling a red dwarf that lies 300 lightyears from Earth. Even with this ship, we'd never make it. Let us not forget it's a used car at this point."

"We go to the closest possible candidate planets in habitable zones with decent atmospheric readings." The James Webb Space Telescope, launched in 2021 to study the atmospheres of exoplanets and look for signs of oxygen, had been doing that for several years. It added immensely to the visual and radiotelescope scans taken of candidate planets within 50 lightyears of Earth. Thankfully, there were several.

"So we'll have two action groups: one working at NASA and in orbit on alien language, ship controls, engines, environmental systems, etc. Also being tasked with misdirecting the normals. They will no doubt breach the second ship as soon as they think they can without blowing the power systems. Our guys there will try to keep that decision at bay while we prepare. Even normals will figure out their language and controls eventually."

Now the floor was held by a young woman almost as tall as these tall men. "The second group, my group, will work on what we need to survive the trip and set up enough of a population for survival in the new world. Those studies have long been done and we'll update them." Pulling out University of Santa Barbara 'Panspermia Task Force' reports from 2020 and 2022, the auburn haired medical student quoted numbers she knew well. "The goal will be 35 mating pairs, 70 individuals to prevent genetic inbreeding problems, but while that ship is big we can hardly be expected to keep 70 of us alive for three decades on it. We must modify its power supply to run our sleeping cargo - just work it, not reinvent it."

"Most fortunate is the innate design of the cockpit. Out translation of raised bumps next to each control indicates a simple auto/manual release. Every control on the bridge is automated, no pilots required. A pilot can assume control of everything or just one thing at a time, then switch back."

"We can fly it".

At several discouraging glances over the idea of running Earth equipment onboard the ship, she offered a perspective. "How many normal Sapiens do you know can build an electric generator? But all of them can plug in an electric light or drive a car. That's us now." The analogy was a good one for this gathering of supremely capable people.

"We'll need life support for our hibernation units, as many as we can, no one older than age 17. Plenty of frozen sperm and egg banks and already fertilized ovum. Incubators. Plenty of robotic nannies, farmers and constructors with 3d support. Gut non-essential alien systems to make room. Space the alien cargo."

There were a few sighs at the waste in what could have been learned if they and not normal sapiens had been the dominant life form of Earth.

"A few robots will be designed to look over our incubators and other biological cargo during the trip. Most robotics will be ground support units, for building a base on the surface before our embryos are decanted. Load up food crop seeds, plus ovum from both fish and small land animals. And us of course. Beneficial farm insects like bees, worms, and cockroaches as well, I'm sorry to say. They are needed." No one laughed at her little joke.

The tall young man continued. "Have everything here ready to go if the hijacking is successful. Load and leave. Install and power up our systems in high Earth orbit if we have to, rather than stay on the ground while we figure it all out. Too dangerous to stay here if they track the ship. And too dangerous to make use of the shuttles found aboard. Shuttle controls are not yet understood as they demand a living pilot, unlike the main vessel which has full autopilot capabilities." This group had breathed a collective sigh of relief when their people in NASA reported that a functioning autopilot had likely made the first ship slide safely into moon orbit. It was working and standing by for orders.

"When ready, land the entire craft somewhere and drop off everyone not in hibernation, and just go."

Thus was an escape plan formulated. Once programmed, the ship flies itself if early indications of translations were reliable. The refitting spent alien stores of liquids and gasses plus Earth equipment required would take liquidation of everyone's assets, and whatever outlying advanced humans could raise. Earth robonauts will be programmed to try waking one person from hibernation on arrival and keep trying one after the other if the first dies. Either way, the ship lands, our robots start building a base, then decant the rest of us inside the grounded ship until the new base is complete. Or complete enough. Start clearing land for farming or building craft for fishing, depending on what the robots find. Anyone awakened can override and modify all the auto procedures if one of us lives thru hibernation. Even wake others if prudent. Otherwise, it's all up to the robots to grow a crop of...us."

As the aliens appeared to have breathed our air, and the dead samples on the first ship were readily identified as being carbon-based eukaryotes, hope held out for human use of at least some of their onboard systems. In addition, to prevent power from being a problem, clever induction sleeves were designed and assembled such that whatever terminals or conduits aboard ship had electrical flow could be tapped, and then used to power Earth equipment. Primitive American farmers had been stealing power from utilities for years using such simple sleeves and induction devices.

The time came for the group to decide to go ahead, whether to risk being found out at NASA or while purchasing/stealing their cargo. To be caught was likely fatal. To be caught as mutants would accelerate the doom of their brethren as well, scattered elsewhere on Earth. Fewer were being caught, but most of those were the youngest. Oddly, the normals had on several occasions identified a gifted one of their own as a mutant and killed it. Killing their own best hopes for survival. They truly deserve to be left behind.

The youngest spoke unbidden about what they were all feeling.

"Chances of waking with current Mars hibernation units stretched from their one-year design to dozens? Another major unknown. I'll take that risk over remaining until the normals hunt us all down. Their DNA testing has become nearly 100% effective. Have you seen the new bill the Senate is passing on tagging us at birth like dogs with subdural chips? Death camps are next and there aren't millions of us to make it messy like Hebrews in Nazi Germany or California with the Japanese. Yeah, I'll take the deep freeze."

Many nods confirmed widespread agreement that this newest version of humanity had no future on this planet.

"Those we don't have enough hibernation units to take should still stay involved with the project. Financial support if nothing else. And the five of us now at NASA rotating up to and down from the project in orbit should no longer be seen with the rest of us assembling our cargo. Two ships came so far, so who is to say more won't be coming? Be ready as you can to try again if the opportunity presents itself."

"This fascist American President isn't about to let foreigners step on his pet project or steal the tech he hopes to get for his military. He'll be busy shielding the American project from foreign leaks, but we're already inside and loyal citizens. The American public at large still knows nothing. That should all work in our favor."

"Most of us never traveled out of the USA, so that's good too. Those that have traveled better dissociate from the rest of us, today, and melt into society. Those well under 21 will be the first ones we notify to try hibernation, so be prepared to travel back here fast and light. Stay close. No contact until then."

"It wouldn't hurt for those on the American project to join one of those online groups who hate or fear mutants or start going to church with the evangelists. Five of us are on the project now, so they should each pick a different 'patriotic' or religious group for improved cover."

The young woman spoke again. "Everyone on the project better keep fresh samples in the fridge of Homo Sapien blood and urine and hair if, no not if, when some bright boy gets the idea to screen the staff for 'mutants'. Once we're tested one time, our five should be "cleared" beyond their already sparkling clean loyalty history. Probably get new clearance badges to wear."

"And no, let's not try to forge ID to get more of us inside. The normals are irrational but not stupid. And very paranoid."

***

So it was that not one but two of the mutant humans on the American project found themselves in orbit with the first team assigned to breach the second ship. Unlike the first, this one exuded power on all wavelengths, and the science team suited up side by side with commandos to try to enter as the aliens would have, without cutting holes in the hull. That may have worked with the first ship because it was so old, powered down, and had no survivors aboard. Even what our biologists called the alien versions of our tardigrades. All were found dead. The bodies and seedlings were being kept quarantined from Earth in orbit.

An airlock was readily identified, not being very different in design from those on the first ship that had to be cut open. There was a pushbutton pad, a lever, and a set of small wheels likely for emergency entry use, as expected. Soon as a clever member of the science team found the proper sequence and cycled the door open, the commandos pushed past and were first thru the hatch.

Also as expected, it was another panspermia ship, loaded with organic cargo. Unlike the first, it appeared to be in the process of launching its cargo towards the Earth but suddenly stopped. The smart money said it was our opening of a hatch that paused deployment. Everyone breathed a sigh of relief that the public wouldn't suddenly see hundreds of alien pods arrivals drifting down thru the atmosphere to land in their back yards. The White House could still control how and when a public announcement was made.

During the next weeks, a routine was established. Commandos remained on the American Station for rapid deployment, especially after several reports of foreign nations bristling that we did not make the entry an international event. Scientists and engineers rotated through the second visitor. Liquid water tanks and recyclers were happily found onboard, encouraging positive comparisons with Earth life, and controls were easily usable by human fingers even if their functions remained a mystery. The designers must have had similar appendages for manipulating their environment.

***

More than one nation had space platforms in Earth orbit, and several had representatives on the International Station. The commandos were ready to secure that station as well. Or destroy it. No one could have anticipated the alien ship suddenly sealing itself one day, then moving out away from Earth as all communications with the onboard science team faded to silent static. The last clear message was that they appeared to have accidentally triggered an autopilot subsystem that was sealing the ship, and were attempting to disable it...when their broadcast was finally cut.

The American Vice President went insane. Began accusing everyone around him of either incompetence or outright disloyalty. Foreign responses were predictable. With the loss of the ship, politicians in every country and their militaries turned their full attention to each other.

A long looping trajectory around the moon followed, then slowly back to one of the Earth/Moon Lagrange points taking several more days. The crew of two did not wish to engage the primary engines, which might be tracked from Earth or even the moon base. Fortunately, alien reactionless maneuvering for use within a solar system was as or more robust than the best action-reaction chemical NASA engines. In dead silence, and with the electromagnetic signature of a piece of coral, they drifted to a stop and waited a full day. Waiting to see if they were detected finally gave them time to dispose of the bodies of the rest of the onboard science team. Regrettable, but this was for species survival. As no radio signals or news from Earth indicated they were being tracked, the ship gradually made its way back to Earth, parking a few dozen miles directly above the cargo team warehouse. The crew used low tech ham radio to check when the cargo would be ready and left again for the same LaGrange point.

Rations they brought were slim but adequate, and not unexpectedly the ship had been found early on to provide potable water. Carbon-based life forms, after all, drank distilled water that was bubble oxygenated. Within 25 days, they returned as planned to land inside the warehouse thru a sliding retractable roof. No alarms appeared to be raised. A night landing without running lights was accomplished by the stealthy alien vessel on reactionless engines.

In less than 36 hours, the youngest nearby members who had been disbursed for having an overseas travel history were contacted and quickly returned singly or in pairs. There were only eight of the Martian hibernation backup units, all they found in NASA storage for future Mars missions. Modification for longer duration began immediately as gear arrived at the warehouse, and the units were already loaded and ready as the ship landed. A neat scam had been used where one NASA contractor facility thought the human freezers were being shipped elsewhere for upgrades and the upgrade contractor knew nothing about it. Too much secrecy kept the various parties from easily checking with each other since, in fact, they were competitor subcontractors. Normals were so amusing sometimes.

Dozens of fertilized eggs are to be grown on arrival. Eight young adults to be woken as needed. And an active crew of several robonauts completed the roster.

The modified units and the balance of cargo were quickly loaded and powered up using very friendly alien and human power couplers. Electricity and magnetism were indeed common ground in science. The logic of positive vs negative and current flow was the same in their world as here. Due to the speed of installation, it would not be necessary to remain safely in orbit while final preparations were made. The ship could leave almost immediately.

Unplanned in the initial meetings, there were three who volunteered to go aboard and remain awake for the takeoff and escape from the solar system. Such was their fatalism on surviving the coming Earth purges. Knowing they would only have dehydrated food for several few weeks, they made the case to the young man and woman leading their operation that while they themselves were theoretically not needed once autopilot was engaged for transit, an unforeseen problem in the first few critical days could make or break the mission. They would stay aboard to monitor and ensure all cargo systems were re-checked and functioning. That amperage and voltage to the incubators and robotic workers were operating well. Sitting in the alien chairs cushioned with human hammock pads, they would continue to pour over alien documents. If they ran out of supplies for themselves, it would be deemed a worthwhile sacrifice to have improved the odds of success that little bit.

The two leaders looked silently at each other, knowing the odds but unable to deny the passion and commitment on display. "There is but a small chance you can get the alien nutrient processors to issue something not inducing vomit. Water is not a problem, and the chemical content of their food seems viable, but cannot yet be stomached." The three teens knew the odds and thought it an even bet with their survival on Earth. Their brethren were now being identified and caught by Homo Sapiens almost weekly. The new American Vice President was efficient and motivated.

If a third alien vessel arrived at this point, few among them believed they could slip past the normals a second time and take control of it.

As their ship left orbit a bloody Earth would soon be too distant to see. The disappearance of the second alien vessel had prompted recriminations from every quarter: That an international crew should have boarded it, as was insisted with the first vessel. That the Americans actually still had the vessel but had stolen and landed it on Earth. That enemies of America had grabbed the vessel, or tried to, and that everyone had lost in a space battle. The final transmission from the science boarding team of an accident notwithstanding, it was more profitable to blame another government than attribute it to bad luck.

Luck for the Earth itself went bad in the first exchanges of tactical nuclear weapons. Whether out of fear of alien technology in American hands or the reverse, weapons long threatened but never used before came to life in overwhelming numbers. Oddly, the collapse of governments in the nuclear ruins might provide mutant survivors a better chance than if Homo Sapien society had managed to hold itself together against them. Irrespective, communities of advanced humans scattered and held out hope. Hope in a single vessel carrying not an alien panspermia mission, but their own. It became a daily exercise to look to the skies wherever they were, once every 23 hours or so when the Earth faced the direction the vessel had taken. Day or night, rain or sun, they faced their direction for a few seconds and sent wishes of speed and deliverance to the ship.

With all the wild normal theories of just what did happen to the second ship, none would come close to describing the truth: three half-starved advanced humans, singing and joking aboard the vessel as they powered up the main engines and passed an old Voyager spacecraft within their Oort cloud on the way to new worlds.

It was a good ship. They christened it the 'Beagle' and etched the name in the ceramics of the command center.

TATTOO WORLD

Mary woke to the usual sounds in her Carolina yard. The recently invading cardinals led the alarm, alerting slumbering mammals to the beginning of another day. Much like the one before, Mary stretched on her back, still lying abed, and took inventory of her aches and pains. At fifty Eridani years of age, roughly 63 Earth years, she knew the common aches and pains of her species. Humans had colonized this moon of the outermost gas giant about the Eridani sun for several hundred years and had become quite acclimated to its lower solar radiation but higher overall electromagnetic radiation fields due to the nearby gas giant itself, Eridani-4.

As part of her morning habit, after checking that she was breathing smoothly and would not pull a muscle in swinging herself to a seated position at the edge of her aluminum composite bed, made of native regolith by 3D printers, she had one more ritual to perform before rising. Her Phoenix.

Raising both arms as her body continued to recline into the softness beneath her, she brought both forearms together where the halves of the odd design resolved themselves into the image she sought. The image she had seen on herself every year since her first menstrual cycle. Not having a moon like on old Earth, the humans and the mammals they brought here were without a gravitational compass to set the needed cycle. A cycle needed not only for regular flushing of old eggs for new but for general health in both males and females. And sanity. For on this world, unlike so many others, humans still had only the two sexes.

Minor odd things occurred to humans as they bred on other worlds, but none as unique as that discovered on this, her homeworld.

She smiled at her Phoenix and slid upward to don her traditional blouse and suit. Short sleeved, of course, as was the custom. Warmth on this world was constant without the seasons of old Earth and provided no need for coats, jackets, or even long sleeve shirts in the evenings. Unlike Earth, the tilt of this world was tidally locked to both its parent planet and its star. Custom had made the baring of the lower arms derringer, almost a taboo to have forearms covered for anything but a broken bone cast or sling.

The marks of her maturity began on her 11th birthday, quite late compared to some of the other girls. Most children knew what was coming. Boys looked forward to their first real hardon. One day, girls would start to grow breasts and hips. And all looked forward to the emergence of their tattoo at about the same time. Until then they followed the human tradition of torturing and taunting anyone different whenever teachers or parents were absent. She knew it was due to her mixed racial heritage. Mother black-Dragon, Father white-Eagle. The tattoos of children of such mixed marriages often did not resolve themselves for several years later than most, so Mary actually considered herself fortunate that the Phoenix she now saw when her forearms came together didn't wait to fully develop until her 18th or 20th birthing day, like some unfortunates of whom cruel rumors abounded. She gazed upon the rampant Phoenix now, still colorfully resplendent after so many decades. Unlike the artificial tattoos humans applied elsewhere in this arm of the galaxy, Eridanis were the only ones fortunate enough to have theirs erupt unbidden and uncontrolled on maturity.

And for most, they never seemed to fade.

Like all genetic traits, they were combinations of both parents and their genetic histories. In the case of such a strongly mixed marriage, still unusual in this century, the combination of the black skin dragon image on one parental side and the white skin eagle image on the other would have unpredictable results in the offspring. Mary was an only child, her mother having lost four previously and had not tried after successfully birthing Mary. No sisters. No brothers.

Or so she thought until last week.

Her aged mother was now stone deaf, and had been since before Mary was born. Eridani was still in many respects a frontier world, but technology had made her mother's deafness a burden but not fatal. Her father having passed into the life of the world twenty years ago, kept close to her mother by video even though her work as a linguist took her afar on this small spinning moon. With one deaf parent and both of such different backgrounds, Mary had grown up with three languages: Esperanto, Swahili, and SouthStarTech-Sign.

Such a beginning foretold her career choices as she found other languages of humans visiting from their worlds to be remarkably simple to assimilate.

Give her a week's hyperwave notice that a dignitary or trade representative would be arriving from Barnard's Star or the Earth asteroid colonies and she would be ready. Lucrative work, but short duration only and often at different spaceports around the globe. Twice she had even been transported to one of the space stations in geosynchronous orbit on the opposite side of Eridani-4.

She never liked being somewhere where she could not see her homeworld in the night sky. But couldn't say no to the bonus credits.

Now she had a comfortable place of her own on the southern half of the northernmost continent. Too far from her mother for efficient ground transport, she, fortunately, had the most advanced video conferencing and sign assist software available. A large 3D panel on the left shows the person at the other end of the call, and a smaller one on the right shows yourself. This was early found to be key to successful signing over the interweb, allowing the 'speaker' to see how he or she appeared and make sure you were not slouching or otherwise out of clear focus. A good signer, like Mary, pulled back further than most to include facial expression, as well as full body language signals, so clear was her hand sign that it could be read at a greater distance than most.

Last week, her mother had excitedly 'called', earlier than the usual time. Being so old, her signing had evolved into an esoteric form that few but her talented daughter could now understand. But even Mary had trouble with this frantic call.

Her Mother knowing her long years were finally winding down, had embarked on a personal mission to wrap up important events in her life. Part of that effort was to obtain new certified copies of Mary's birth certificate, and those of the children she had lost at or near birth. Her excitement came when the last one arrived, the one for the son who she swore to Mary had lived a week before expiring.

Eridani was harsh on the human reproductive cycle. Each generation was getting better adapted, but it was still a struggle to breed a full complement of replacements. If not enhanced by new colonists, the population would be slowly dwindling. Instead, it could recently boast a modest but steady growth.

Mary's mother went on and on about how the doctors, most in those days racially white-eagle or black-lion, told her that her son had failed to survive and sent her home a week after the birth. Yet the certificate she now held in her hand, the sealed and stamped official record, showed her son died at birth like the other three! Outrageous, she claimed. In those days, doctors routinely took children from "certain" families if the genetic marker looked promising and sold them to those with wealth and power. Especially those couples who couldn't conceive at all. Few worlds had the pressure to reproduce found back then on Eridani. All worlds still held the ancient human traits of selfishness, greed, and prejudice as justification for atrocities.

Her son might be alive, she inaudibly screamed, gesturing wildly while faxing the obviously contradictory document for Mary to see for herself. Her mother's Dragons flashed across the three dimensional screen, seeming to take flight in her anger. Mary could remember as a child being told she had a brother, if only for a week. It wasn't only the ravings of a fading octogenarian, but something she remembered her father confirming those few times they spoke of it years ago when he was alive. If the certificate was wrong about him living a week, he could have easily lived more than that. He could be alive today, went her claim.

Mary managed to calm her down, and in the succeeding week had performed the usual phone calls and received the usual stonewalling when authorities found out what she was interested in. Even if nothing had occurred, just the suggestion that such a thing happened at "their" institution caused an immediate lockdown from every agency and organization and physician involved. She then hit on the idea of using the entertainment show, "The Seekers", which was produced in the Earth asteroid belt but seen weeks or months after it originally aired live on all outer human colonies. As much as we might have changed physically in our expansion into the galaxy, humans still loved watching shows about the lives of other humans, especially shows where far flung relatives or adopted children sought out family. Family members which might now reside in multiple worlds. Other than the Interworld Olympics, these kinds of shows might come and go but always reappeared successfully in a slightly new form.

The orbital glider ride to her mom in the north was uneventful. Mary spent it remembering her life as an only child. Half of her friends growing up were also only children. She remembered wondering what her tattoo would look like considering her parentage. The other children knew about it, of course, and teased her about what kind of gory abomination would emerge on her arms. Or perhaps a mishmash, some said, with no real form or design. She remembered crying alone in the school bathroom, wanting her older brother to have lived, to be there for her now, to stop the bullying and stand beside her, no matter what design came out. She looked at her young bare arms then and almost willed them to be her mother's Dragon or father's Eagle. Her skin was blackish brown in shading, so she supposed it would more closely resemble her mother, and she never did find out her almost brother's skin color as an indicator of which way his tattoo might appear.

Some days, she dreaded the eruption of the image as a cancer of her own body betraying her.

One year several of her teachers had explained to her the science behind why tattoos occurred to those conceived and born here on Eridani. How it followed the parental tattoos, as in variations on trees or lions or other living archetypes, though no one knew quite why. Furthermore, it was known they displayed in such a way that foretold the disposition of the owner. In the first generations, it had seemed a coincidental thing, but after several generations on the planet, it was clear that the colors and beauty or anger and darkness of the tattoo foretold much of the owner. It seemed to be an increasingly accurate marker with each generation. Sociopaths and sadists were now found out early, sometimes before they themselves knew what those terms meant. Treatments and counseling were instituted in such cases, and unlike in other worlds where therapeutic results would never be certain, here the tattoos themselves would slowly alter as the disposition of the owner was altered from the random pathways their genetics had directed them.

The modification of the tattoos from the inside out was slow, taking years, but astonishing. In adults who had received strong trauma, like the loss of a loved one by violence, the reverse was also found to be true. Fifth generation Eridanis would find their colors unaccountably muted by tragedies, and brightened by each successfully birthed child or grandchild. There was great hope that in time, Eridani would become the only human world that could claim a level of social peace and safety from our fellow man unknown anywhere else in the galaxy.

But of course, there was another side.

Stasis had not yet occurred in their world. Tattoos were weaker and less predictive in the newer generations. There was snobbery and racism. And of course, those who wished to disguise their family heritage could always find those who could help them. Those who made their living performing nose and eye plastic surgery. Those who would bleach or color your skin. And of course, those who created tattoos the old fashioned way, with needle and ink. The technology was prohibited, of course, but only high tech laser treatments could easily be proscribed and tracked. The centuries-old needle and ink were simple tools, simply hidden, and found in the back alleys where humans had always hidden the darker desires of their hearts.

Of course, there were legitimate tattoo parlors run by the government, where people went to embellish their natural forearm images by adding other related images on their shoulders, legs, neck, or backs, to complement their family tattoo. But for the right amount of money, and if you didn't mind the primitive technique of the needle, anything could be added. Even disguising or altering your natural heritage. There was a brisk market for criminals from off world as well, stowaways or those with money, who came with naked arms and soon had found someone to alter their appearance to look native Eridani.

Mary arrived at her mother's house at the same time as the local "The Seekers" video crew. They would film an interview with her mother, with Mary herself translating, and send the raw footage to the Earth asteroid colony for final processing. The crew was quite encouraging, in that her mother's lifelong deafness and mixed racial background would be titillation points in their favor during the selection process. And the stolen/sold baby angle had the film crew very excited. Even at a blistering three 1-hour shows per day, there were thousands more applicants than time to air them all. Still, they were encouraged that something could be done while her mother yet lived.

As they sat side by side, her mother signing slowly as age made itself known, Mary half listened and half studied the Dragon variation belonging to her mother. She periodically looked at videos of her father now and then to remind her of how his Eagle had been so bold and rampant, such an iconoclast was he. She wondered as she sat just what a brother would have looked like had he lived long enough. While smiling and nodding for her mother to keep her calm, Mary herself did not believe he was taken or yet lived. She had no siblings. Her aloneness would be complete after her mother passed. Still, such things as baby theft were a lot more common in those days of infertile couples…

Months passed and their show was finally aired. Mary sat at home this time, signing by interweb with her mother and comforting her that now that at least there was an active video record of both her mother and father's tattoos out among the worlds. That if someone was born with one of them but of the 'wrong' corresponding skin color, or perhaps had a mottled combination of the two family icons like Mary did in her fortunately clear but unique Phoenix, and always wondered at where they came from, that they might now know. Perhaps her brother bore a Griffin, unknown among the families but a logical combination of Eagle and Dragon. Perhaps, but no, this was just a final kindness to her dying mother. A hope after years without hope for the continuance of the family.

Mary herself had tried but could not bear children. Her unique Phoenix was at times painful for her to bear among her fellow man, but she had learned to bear it proudly and now genuinely took pleasure in it. Even used it to differentiate herself to off-world clients who were uniformly enchanted by her lovely and vividly colored icon; a single violet head with flashing tongue, one wing folded forward protectively, one outstretched with brilliant yellow talons reaching to its left, a breast of layered blue mica colored plates, with strong legs beneath, sheathed in large yellow feathers.

After her mother joined her father, having lived a full life and done everything she could to give that sense of family to her only daughter, Mary picked up her own life and had all but forgotten the episode. Neighbors talked about it incessantly for weeks, but eventually, it lost its interest to new scandals or celebrity events. One day the usual tone came to the monitor, the one that announced another off-world arrival next month who would request her services. She sat before the screen, acknowledged the contract, then pushed back more than the common distance to allow herself to be shown at full height.

Clicking it on after confirming the hyperwave link had been established, the screen slowly resolved, but it wasn't the businessman or politician she expected to negotiate fees with. The man was too casually dressed. He was sitting comfortably on a large couch and he was not alone. A woman Mary assumed was his wife sat on the arm of the couch, leaning in with one arm around his neck, grinning broadly. Restlessly sitting on the floor in front of them were five young people of varying ages but clearly their offspring. Only lastly did she notice their common family trait. Though his wife had the lovely bare arms of off-world humans and Eridani children, the man bore a striking pair of tattoos on both forearms. And each of the five children also bore nearly identical markings.

At the distance needed to see them all in one frame, Mary found herself leaning forward, struggling to understand what it was she beheld. It was moments before she leapt off the ground as the man and the five children each brought their own forearms together and the images resolved into the left and right brilliant yellows and blues of a Phoenix.

She knew then that she was no longer alone in the universe.

SEED SHIP

"So the funding came in?" For this? That last he did not voice. His voice was hopeful but somewhat incredulous. For some weeks he had been encouraging in a backhanded way. After all, with all the problems of the world in this century and how tight money was for pure theoretical research, a scientist like him could be forgiven a little for doubting money would be spent on a project like this one. Her project.

The very idea that mankind should begin remotely placing life on other planets, farther afield than our solar system, had plenty of opponents. NASA and the Euro space agencies, the old Soviet Russians as well, had spent considerable energy in their space efforts to prevent contaminating heavenly bodies with Earth based organics, right down to germs and bacterium. Almost as much effort as they spent decontaminating and quarantining early astronauts until they were certain the reverse had not occurred.

Known as panspermia, the theory that life could be transplanted by natural processes from planet to planet or even farther had begun in recent years to gain some traction. The question of whether we should intentionally undertake such activities gained adherents after Antarctic expeditions discovered pieces of Mars in the permafrost during the late 20th century. Some contained questionable evidence of Martian organic compounds if not life.

Jacob looked fondly at Freya's still beautiful face, one which he once woke up to in years past, and with whom he now only shared scientific interests. He had blown it, he knew in his bones, to have lost this wonderfully unique feminine creature of beauty and intelligence, but was somewhat satisfied to be involved in at least part of her life. It was enough.

His former lover found his initial lack of enthusiasm over the news disappointing. Only a few weeks earlier Freya put in a proposal for a panspermia study as part of her teaching duties as an introductory astronomy professor. This was more of an answer than she could have imagined. Betraying no expression, she did not want to alienate one of the few engineers of her acquaintance who did not openly dismiss or discourage her ideas in general and this one in particular. A woman scientist was still in a minority at this time in human history and she consoled herself with knowing that with all its flaws, America was one of those countries where a woman like her, who evoked feelings of lust at first sight, could at least try to have a career as something other than a trophy wife or entertainer.

Freya explained how the representative of a philanthropist had approached her and several in her department at USC Santa Barbara for interest. Sitting in on one of her lectures while a visiting professor in astronomy at neighboring Santa Barbara college, after reading of her career accomplishments online and her other eclectic interests, this industrialist had thought her the right person to initiate a project for intentional panspermia. To spread carbon-based life off the Earth into the universe at large.

The University had forwarded her a copy of his offer, essentially a free hand in direction and accomplishments. Total lack of University oversight. And a little hard for them to swallow, with no potential deliverables which the University might claim and profit from. Highly unusual for outside funding. Corporations doing so usually had strict guidelines and milestone requirements, sharing the fruits of labor including patents with the University, as well as tight oversight. This individual understood the extremely distant nature of anything which could be characterized as 'success'. The lack of obvious profit for the University was glaring.

The team met quietly with little fanfare. Even her favorite grad students and personal assistants had little idea what was up.

"Our potential benefactor had provided a preliminary paper, unsourced, outlining a purely robotic mission outside our solar system. Four or Five android units with specific areas of expertise. A single vessel to be sent as soon as the technologies mature, destination Wolf-1. Other vessels to follow at 10-year intervals or so to other nearby star systems with habitable zone planets, funding permitting.

"From this modest outline and excel spreads, it will be our task to (a) determine the required technologies and techniques, (b) collect required technologies currently available, and (c) invent-discover-or wait for those gaps which are apparent in our efforts. This could take decades."

There was a collective sigh and dropping of shoulders around the conference table. The invited team consisted of two others like herself from astronomy and physics, two others from biology with backgrounds in previous biodome experiments here on Earth, and of course Jacob. The engineer. The nuclear engineer at a time when students and professors alike were violently protesting against his chosen field of study. His experience creating devices and robotic remotes for the nuclear industry would certainly come in handy, as well as his longstanding love of science fiction novels.

It occurred to her that she knew Jacob far better than her other colleagues, and such peripheral knowledge from teammates might reveal unexpected dividends. She admonished herself to go beyond her comfort zone and become better acquainted outside their obvious academic qualifications and interests.

"I hereby propose we all study this strawman paper and further propose we are each assigned to specific areas in line with the original AI robots and their teleoperated extensions proposed by this benefactor."

There were considered nods around the table, as those present were dimly considering why they even wanted to be part of this effort. After all, it was an open-ended project, with a termination at success likely past the end of their careers, perhaps their lifetimes. Their efforts at best would be a detailed plan at the limits of current, and even projected, technologies and knowledge of life itself and evolution. Closer to well documented science fiction than science. Succeeding generations of scientists, if any, would be the ones to see its fruition - if ever - after perhaps generations of improvements and discoveries until such journeys were feasible. They all had other concerns than pure science, especially their careers.

The light in her eyes told Jacob she was already committed. He could see the hesitation and doubts on the others around the table, even if she could not, and decided on the spot to go it alone with her if necessary. He told himself it was the kind of challenge he wanted after his semi-retirement which he lied to himself was the reason for his quick decision and not unresolved affection for the stunning 65-year-old before him. Did she not age at all? Did the years really not change her open joyful outlook on life or essential decency?

After the meeting, he delayed her in the hallway. "Thanks for getting me a copy of the preliminary before the meeting. I already have a few additions to the plan with current technologies or techniques the author or authors seem unaware. Do you think it was put together by our benefactor himself?" And quickly added, "Or herself?"

"I haven't asked. It doesn't matter to me. It is really here. A chance to do this. Or at least start it. A beginning that will be added to and added to over the years until we figure it out. Until we as a species get ourselves off this fragile planet."

"If we last that long. The way things are going sometimes…but then again that's the point, isn't it? Others are working on Martian, Lunar, or asteroid belt colonization, but that may be even further out than this, timewise."

"Oh, I'm certain of it. So much has been done with robotic craft already, tough as that is, as you yourself know even better than I, but the idea we could send humans in sufficient numbers and create an entire independent colony seems more and more impossibly distant to me. I don't know if we, humans, will make it that far." That last was spoken softly, with unaccustomed sadness in her otherwise light, feminine voice. They both were well aware of the phosphorus rarity problem and how unusually rich in this essential element was Earth.

"Wow", he commented, "I never thought I'd hear you be pessimistic about humans finding a way, for the decent among us to overcome our baser instincts and overcome those who would see half the world burn as long as they got to be in charge of the remains. But I'm with you. We should get something of life out there. You know I've always believed the universe is chock full of life. But what if I'm wrong? What if two planets collided, one water, one iron cored, forming the Earth and Moon system is the kind of rare phenomena required for truly complex life like us? Perhaps there are only plants or algae out there. Perhaps nothing. Perhaps there was nothing here but plants until we got seeded by a panspermia event like some extremists think."

He paused, trying not to just stare at her and lose his train of thought. She still was that 19-year-old girl he met so long ago. He fumblingly thought he often sounded like a bumper sticker when around her but said out loud anyway, "If we truly are all there is, it is a moral responsibility to seed the universe."

She gave him a rare radiant smile, saying "Or at least our little corner of one medium size galaxy. It would be nice to be part of the progress of science. You and I will never win a Nobel, or get rich, but maybe, just maybe, we can start something really important here. I'm going to try. Say, how about enlisting some of my graduate students to perform specific subtasks. They'd be cheap and creative, and we need both."

"Sure," he responded, "which means one of our first tasks will be to organize tasks, to create a...punch list, to use an engineering construction term, to make a very specific set of tasks which can be distributed to experts, or students, with knowledge in specific areas without believing in or even seeing the project as a whole. Then a PERT chart to track the remaining holes in our knowledge."

"But of course," she added, "certain tasks will require overall project knowledge, a gestalt of several disciplines. And spreading knowledge of the goal of the project and publicity overall will certainly provide unplanned benefits."

"That's where we come in. We can start to flesh out the paper ourselves in all areas, and should I think get the process organized to how we add and review new potential inclusions. I mean, before we start the work itself. Then begin bringing in the kids or outside experts. We can start it, but should ultimately end up as information managers. This is a long effort. Not only is no one alive capable of putting it all together now, but the details will be more than any one mind can hold, except at an executive summary level. The further along we get, I'm afraid the fewer and fewer will be our individual contributions to the whole."

She stopped walking and gave him a look. "Are you claiming prescience or divine inspiration?" Her jib was well received, as he knew she knew him to be without superstitions or deities.

"No, not prescience. Just remembering what records of the Manhattan Project say, and that was a very immediate effort of the best people anyone could ask for. More like the crash program to go to the Moon, years and thousands of contributors large and small, or Asimov's Foundation trilogy." They'd both read him and enjoyed it, though he knew her to be more of a LeGuin 'Earthsea' enthusiast. This would not just be a hobby to either of them. Or a resume enhancement, common enough in the publish-or-perish nature of modern university science. It made him wonder more about their benefactor.

What could possibly motivate someone ready to commit 5 million dollars over the next five years, to be followed by twice that much in the next five, with a balloon trust of 135 million dollars available from which actual construction models and tests could be performed. Who was this guy? Then again, how many billions had been spent by the rich boys like Musk and Branson and Bezos. For all they accomplished, many still put their achievements down to boys measuring their toys with each other.

As he fell asleep that night, he thought he'd like his focus to take the part of the deployment. The paper talked about a variety of re-entry vehicles tailored to various gravity fields and atmospheric densities. Designs inspired by dandelions, maple tree polywogs, and low mass low speed unpowered balloon-saucer designs. And various payloads. Spores, sponges, seaweed, and everything from cyan bacteria to tardigrades. Still, he mused, R-DEPLOY would likely fall into the hands of one of the biologists, claiming it as dealing directly with their expertise, with someone like himself being relegated to R-SHIP, either design or maintenance or both. Engines and power supply and navigation. That could be immensely gratifying, for an unmanned trip spanning over a dozen lightyears. And the onboard AI programs which would run the ship once away from Earth, direct its maintenance, and decide if and when and how to begin seeding around one or more target worlds. For this to work, they had to be autonomous.

But as he lost consciousness that night he found himself readying arguments for him to be involved intimately in the design and operation of soft landing deployment vehicles for everything from bacteria and plant seeds to small insects and animals. He smiled in the dark.

Jacob found himself surprised that the conference table was once again full, but less surprised that the faces had all changed. While all of her original invitees had explained in one way or another how they wished to bow out, she was comforted that they had spread the word and a full set had showed up in their place. Same fields, and just what she thought the project needed to begin.

Explaining the original paper which they had all by now read, she thought a top to bottom discussion of what was there so far would be beneficial. Her approach to them was clear: to assume they had been commanded to build the ship and stock it today. What was needed?

Distances and technological limits are such that sending humans is inefficient and presently impractical, and would likely be for a century to come. Launch a robotic piloted vehicle to the nearest likely star system. The paper noted Wolf-1 with several 'rocky' planets identified the size of Earth. A robotic AI will crew the ship, each with a specialty and under a central commanding AI; from experience, he approved wholeheartedly multiple AI control as opposed to a single entity controlling everything. Sufficient quantities of primitive life forms would be deployed on worlds depending upon local conditions, including bacteria, asexual creatures, plants, animals, water-based, land-based, and even some forms designed and engineered by human geneticists to fill expected niches or improve viability.

The scope was inspiring to this room of scientists who grew up with quantum mechanics math often beyond their understanding, in a world where simple core technological devices were already invented and developed. They loved but often tired of teaching the new generation and wanted to be scientists of the unknown again, as they uniformly did in their youth. The astronomers among them immediately saw the onboard application of the automated NGIS transit planet search array, being highly autonomous and largely unmanned. It would yield good practices and procedures for their pilotless missions into deep space.

She continued the briefing with the set of excel spreadsheets that had accompanied the paper.

The DECISION TREE listed a series of databases and tables to be referenced by the logic engines: perform IF-THEN-ELSE decisions for conduct of the mission. They could not assume having AIs which were conscious, a dream still unachieved. Arguments appeared familiar to the trained programmers present. Tables of data would be populated before leaving Earth and will be updated by sensor readings and samplings onboard as they approach candidate systems.

LIFEFORMS was a master database with specific information on each lifeform taken for seeding, including their best matching environmental conditions and delivery methods. The biologists among them jumped in and were already debating what forms could survive the journey and be revived or cultivated using a robotic nanny. The discussion of what could live in which environment was cut short as Freya loved but corralled their enthusiasm for now.

ENVIRONMENTS outlined but did not yet populate a master database of several standard environmental types, which if identified in the field will determine which life forms to be cross-referenced having known compatibility with the environs found. Four samples for Mars, Earth, Venus, and the moon Encedalus were included as templates. Each world studied will have a custom environmental table populated with local data and data ranges as the ship approaches, and match life forms from that database. They were beginning to appreciate the thought that the anonymous author(s) had put into this project. It was clearly intended to be practical and achievable, and not simply an academic exercise.

Robot-CTRL Subroutines were defined as primary subroutines called upon to decide if and when and how to take action for operational responsibilities. Each subroutine will call several generic procedures specific to certain related tasks. The imagined generic procedure list could easily number a thousand. Or ten times more.

Robot-MAINT Subroutines were defined as, once again, primary subroutines called upon to decide on if and when, and how to take action for maintenance responsibilities. Each subroutine will call several generic procedures specific to certain maintenance tasks. These would include parts replacement using hot spares and manufacturing parts using onboard 3-D printers and a variety of stock materials. The AI units themselves at the top of the controls hierarchy would have two RAID backups each, not a new technology but proven. Though specializing in maintenance or deployment or whatever, each could be uploaded from another backup if that primary robot was destroyed or otherwise disabled by radiation or aging on the trip. R-Maint would also remotely control the mobile robots aboard.

Robot-COMM Subroutines would be called upon to decide on if and when and how to take action for long distance surveillance and navigational responsibilities. Each subroutine will call several generic procedures specific to sensory input and decision making tasks. They would not expect to find a ready made biosphere that they could then populate. This mission was predicated on the idea that conditions for life were common, but the presence of life itself might very well be rare or unique to Earth. If the reverse was true, and Earth's Orion Arm of the Milky Way galaxy was heavily populated with life at all levels of development, then the SETI style broadcasts of R-COMM might find an audience as they traveled there.

Robot-DEPLOY Subroutines were planned to decide if and when and how to take action for lifeform deployment responsibilities once in system. Each subroutine will call several generic procedures specific to final surveys of a planetary body before deployment, identification of matching geographical areas to the life forms on board, and only then initiating numerous small drops using the appropriate entry vehicles. Knowing large masses would burn up without retrorockets and heat shields, and thinking chemical rockets would likely not survive the interstellar journey still viable, the mass of the largest vehicle would have to be small enough to use parachutes and natural aerodynamics to slow their descent. Packages of thousands of bacteria carriers shaped like dandelions, polliwog shaped seed carriers which would helicopter from orbit to the surface and decay open; ballooned pods were envisioned which could land in oceans or other large water bodies and burst open pounds of contents.

Jacob thought about someone's suggestion of dropping loads of shuttlecocks with seeds or other payloads onto land or ocean from high orbit. If released from a sled moving backward against orbital velocity, they would enter an atmosphere at essentially 0 m/sec vertical and due to high drag, never heat up as the atmosphere thickened, never reaching high speeds. He liked the idea for all their deployment craft if they could work out a disposable reliable retro sled design. For himself, he was fondest of the saucer-shaped spinners, among all these passive unguided vehicles, which reminded him of a childhood toy he made with friend Ed Carlino which was mostly curved vanes held inside a perimeter circle and fired spinning from a pistol launcher: these would simply be dropped at low orbit and could be sized to carry a variety of payloads including a sensor lander with onboard miniature rovers and drones to perform ground-based analysis just before landing the first biological payload. If he and Ed had been more entrepreneurial as children, it would have been they who invented the Frisbee.

At the next meeting, everyone at the table remembered the dismay when the Viking missions analyzed Martian soil and found it compound rich but poisonous to Earth plants and animals in its present state, not to mention ambient solar radiation levels. Someone remembered the army's Multi Utility Tactical Transport (MUTT) by GDLS. If they modified theirs with inflatable balloons on its legs, like that Vonnegut story, it could traverse land and water in exploration as well as drop life forms in the best locations found. Just make the 4 hoofed legs concave in the back for a dog paddle if needed. They figured quickly that the balloon displaced volume on 4 legs could float up to 200kg, so theirs must be lighter than the existing army MUTT.

Robot-SHIP consisted of descriptions of a potential primary vessel, seeding deployment vessels, and all required systems for extended autonomous operations. Most of the members deferred to engineer Jacob here, as their experience with power systems and vehicle construction was not just weak, but largely absent. They all knew that surviving known in system radiation levels and gravitational stress had made the success of Voyager surviving into the local Kuiper Belt one of that mission's highlights. He thought the plan for a central ship intelligence controlling navigation and environment was sound, then tasked R-MAINT to conduct repairs using its teleoperated remotes. This separation would lose nothing in translation while providing the required discipline focus and redundancies.

Assignments were made without much dissent. There was plenty of work for everyone in their own most desired areas of interest. Three went with R-DEPLOY, two to R-MAINT, and surprisingly three wanted R-COMM. Jacob on R-SHIP and Freya herself took a first cut at R-CTRL. R-MAINT would need more hands, but for a first cut, fewer people were thought better to more fully develop an initial program of equipment, procedures, and priorities. Two of the members had studied the lessons learned documents coming out of BioDome I and II, as Jacob had from the Three Mile Island disaster, and were anxious to apply those lessons here. They would meet bimonthly to start, then stay flexible in their human framework.

Soon enough, specific tasks and procedures and programming needs would be identified and distributed to either interested professionals or, no less interested, graduate students looking for something in which to sink their teeth for padding their University studies with experience. A young programmer, Fred West, not present at the initial meetings, approached Jacob when he saw the flyers posted around campus. He had to believe an autonomous robotic mission, far more so than primitive Voyager or teleoperated Vikings and Mars rovers, would need him. Basic, Fortran, Visual C++, and Prolog were his to command. Jacob had to agree and soon they were discussing Linux specifics far in advance of where the project stood at this nascent beginning.

Jacob took a mental step back and tried to steer the discussion the same way he and Freya had, to see the big control picture before bogging down in details. The young programmer grasped the need to decide the nature of the onboard robotic 'society' they sought to create. Not able to anticipate every event, AI was assuredly required at every level. At the top, they now decided that 5 robotic artificial life (RAL) units would need to communicate and somehow jointly decide on courses of action.

West immediately felt insect NEMS would be the way to go. Single minded creatures. Hardcoded programming of tasks, tasks which they and their robotic remotes would perform or die trying. Yet communal in the overall result. Jacob countered with thoughts of small primitive human communal living groups. One strong leader, everyone knowing their job and toeing the line, with verbal communication very basic and of limited vocabulary. They immediately agreed the multitude of complex human communication gestures and expressions would have to be omitted despite good work being done there by the Japanese and gladly lost the complexities of an associated emotional basis. The equivalent of hardcoded instincts of a reptilian amygdale would be enough. Pursuing that came to a military manner of obedience, order giving, and questioning performed by first questioning whether they can ask a question! The military mindset believed in the department of redundancy department for orders.

'So we're looking at a framework which combines insect instincts with military discipline and control from the top, huh?" said an introspective West. "Write everything to fit somewhere in that kind of community. Neat.

It would be decades before their work saw fruition.

In the interim, Jacob sought to fix at least the engine portion of the design. This would enable him to focus more on ship power systems and redundancies. And the fascinating AI control systems West was working on. Clever kid, that West.

He explained to Freya that if they want to complete the trip within, say, 20 years, the ship would have to travel at 21% of the speed of light. Then slow down at the destination. This means that we need a way to accelerate up to 21% of the speed of light, and then slow down back to zero - the deltaV sum is 42% of the speed of light. That's far too much for chemical.

"It sounds right. Too much fuel to carry is the limiting factor?"

"Oh yeah. Using the Tsiolkovsky rocket equation, we can work out the ratio between the propellant and non-propellant masses of the rocket we are using. You would need more than the entire mass of the universe, like 10^{53} kg. Chemical rockets for relativistic travel are *beyond* impractical. And nothing short of relativistic speeds will get our ship somewhere before it falls apart with age."

"What about nuclear rockets, your old specialty?" She remembered fondly their days together with both of them as science majors, learning about life at the same time.

"Ok. I repeated the calculation for effective exhaust velocity of a nuclear photon rocket."

"1 kg/s of fusion fuels are consumed, for a power output of 353 TW. This produces 2,235.6 kN of thrust out of a 95% efficient emitter. We expel 996.1 grams per second of waste, so the effective exhaust velocity is 2,244.4 km/s. This is nearly five times more than NASA estimates for a fission photon rocket's effective exhaust. The reality is that a plausible fusion photon rocket with a mass ratio of 100 would only have a deltaV of 10,335 km/s or 3.4% of the speed of light. Barely enough for a multiple century generation ship to cross the stars and certainly not enough for travel within a lifetime or two. Staging the fusion rocket will not help very much. Even a photon rocket is very inefficient.

Freya responded, "So what's the alternative? Leave the choice of engine to the future?"

He smiled knowingly. "Actually we have an old technology which simply hasn't been used in our haste to launch satellites and ICBMs with chemical rockets. A thermionic heat engine. The range of a rocket must work for at least 16-20 lightyears, whatever duration it takes. Likely a century or more. That allows our seed ship to theoretically reach planets located in 42 star systems. The ecosphere exists on maybe a dozen planets located within this gigantic radius. We should plan flights to planets with an exosphere in the system of stars Alpha Centauri,

Proxima A, Tau Cetus, and the Gliese system. How to get there turns out to be kind of simple.

In a traditional nuclear photonic rocket, an onboard nuclear reactor would generate such high temperatures that the blackbody radiation from the reactor would provide significant thrust. The disadvantage is that it takes much power to generate a small amount of thrust this way, so acceleration is very low. The photon radiators would most likely be constructed using graphite or tungsten. Photonic rockets are technologically feasible but rather impractical with current technology based on an onboard and very complex nuclear reactor power source expected to survive all those years." He shook his head. "Not a chance for a fission reactor."

"Thermionics then. Direct conversion of heat to energy. Whereas the full "active" reactor system in a nuclear thermal rocket can be expected to generate over a gigawatt, a radioisotope generator might get only 5-10 kW. But no moving parts to wear out or require maintenance. This means that the design of devices already built for the arctic and orbital power, while highly efficient, can produce thrust levels of perhaps only 1.3 to 1.5 N, making them useful only for thrusters. To increase the power for medium duration missions, our engines would typically use fuel with a short half-life such as Po-210, as opposed to the typical RTG which would use a long half-life fuel such as plutonium-238 (87-year half-life) to produce a more constant power over longer periods. The even shorter half-life element fermium has also been suggested.

"Does the half-life matter, as long as it's still enough to get where we want, say systems within 20 lightyears?"

"Oh yeah." He warmed to explaining the differences in energy expenditure from natural radioactive decay, like in the old days of their youth. "As a rough estimate, atoms tend to give off 1/1000th of their mass and energy over a half-life. Something like Uranium-235 produces so little energy from half-life decay, like 700,000 years, that you could safely hold it in your hand. Milliwatts only, but for a billion years. A half-life in the hundreds of years gives off kilowatts instead. Take PO-210 with a half-life of 139 days pours out its energy much faster. It's an alpha emitter as well, so no hard gamma to shield.

"So that's the fuel? The alpha particles?"

"Not...really. Not like a chemical propellant based on the action/reaction exhaust of gases. A photon rocket propulsion produces thrust via the emission of intense light from heating a surface. Infrared. Light has pressure, like on a spinning desktop radiometer toy. So no massive propellant is required, lightening the ship and vastly improving the cargo to engine ratio. Plus remember, no reactor with moving parts to fail."

"While photons do not have mass, they do still carry linear momentum and so create a small reaction force when emitted or absorbed. Even without an exhaust, the photon pressure of the energy emitted by a thermal source can produce thrust, although an extremely tiny amount. A famous example of spacecraft thrust due to photon pressure was the Pioneer anomaly, in which photons from the onboard radioisotope source caused a tiny but measurable acceleration of the Pioneer spacecraft. Drove NASA nuts until they figured it out. A similar phenomenon occurred on the New Horizons spacecraft; photons (thermal infrared) from the RTG, reflected from the spacecraft's antenna, produced a very small thrust which propelled the spacecraft slightly off course! We would use that as our primary accelerator." He loved the idea of no moving parts.

"It was enough to push those ships off course?", she asked with her usual genuine curiosity.

"Oh yeah, the first actual case of photonic heat propulsion was accidental."

"It's not fast, in fact, the slowest space system I've come across, but it keeps accelerating and can reach nearby star systems in centuries instead of millennia. There's a pair of old patents we can look at to see the tech is super easy to engineer." He looked on his phone for notes for a moment, then texted her "United States Patent 3315471; Direct cycle radioisotope rocket engine; 1967 and Patent 3306045; Radioisotope rocket; 1967.

"You think this is the best? Right now the one to beat?"

He nodded in affirmation. "Sure, there's the Nuclear Photonic Rocket (NPR) and the Antimatter Photonic Rocket (APR) first proposed in the 1950s. Even the idea of setting off atomic bombs - small ones - one after another in pulses behind a large shield on the back of your ship. That could move tons of colonization cargo, people and all, but nobody has done it." He hastened to add, "Though the engineering has been tested and works.

Freya laughed out loud. "Atomic bombs popping out the back? That's a joke, right? You'd destroy the Earth under you! Minimum!"

"No, no it's for real. I've seen videos of chemical versions. In fact, it's the only propulsion system we have right now with no new engineering that can launch the tons required for a human colony in another solar system. They can be as big as aircraft carriers, and even more expensive! Now solar sails operate on the same principle as photon rockets, deriving thrust from the tiny transfer of momentum that occurs when photons are emitted from a surface or bounce off of a reflector, but cannot move much mass. The key difference is that a solar sail depends on an external light source, and its maneuverability is limited by the direction of that light source, while a photon rocket carries its own light source along with it. I've even seen ideas for harnessing a black hole or bending space around the front and rear of a ship for warp drive, but nothing we've built is known to work yet for a large colony ship but pulse bombs. Yet."

She interjected into his obvious excitement at this idea. "I remember reading about the broomsticks from Donald Moffet's science fiction novel 'The Jupiter Theft'. They used photon rockets powered by mass/energy conversion with a high enough power output to produce a full g of acceleration. At that intensity, the energy density in the exhaust beam led to particle/antiparticle pair production, making the beam visible from the side. Very clever. And lovely."

Nodding again, and appreciating the sheer breadth of her intellect for the thousandth time, "I've built a model for ours based on the old designs using PO-210, but without the polonium of course. A sphere of PO-210 is suspended behind a parabolic reflector. The sphere is encased in tungsten graphite, which is heated by itself via isotopic decay to emit infrared radiation. The parabolic reflector is designed to reflect infrared frequencies. Half the output is lost in non-collimated exhaust out the back, and some of the radiation hitting the reflector is lost at the extreme edges as well. This can be improved by placing the PO-210 in a sphere of conductive but non-radiating metal on the exhaust side, and only the reflector side has the tungsten graphite.

"So does the tungsten graphite boil off as propellant?"

No, no. Just glows in infrared and the photons emitted are the sole 'propellant'.

"I'd like to see your math. Everyone is building reusable chemical rockets these days, and ion or nuclear drives for within a solar system. Not thermionic. But if the math holds up, we can set the idea aside until someone comes up with an improved low maintenance and high-speed answer."

"High ultimate speed. From my power equations, it moves as slow as a pig in a mud pile for the first few years but can reach the closest star systems in centuries. And best of all, it's tech we have right now. Can be built tomorrow in my garage. If we don't mind the radiation hazard.

If and when we come up with better practical interstellar engines, fine. But until then, this is it." He started ticking off points on his fingers. "It does not require tons of propellant like chemical or nuclear rockets, starts slower than ion rockets, but does not require a massive nuclear reactor and so mostly ship and payload. It would be launched with conventional rockets or another launch assist system best at the time, then discard the chemical stage entirely when out of Earth's gravity, say past the orbit of the moon. We would need a separate power source, likely nuclear, to generate ship power but that will still be far smaller than a nuclear engine ship. Power would likely be augmented when in-systems by solar panels as well."

"Ship power is likely where I'll be putting most of my energy as it's a harder problem than propulsion. First, we need to keep iterating the amount of power we need. 10kwe? 1Mwe? That will tell me what power systems exist that can fill the need. Huge fission reactors at 1000 MWe are out of the question, and fusion reactors don't exist, so I'll start with SMRs, small modular reactors. There are dozens of designs, all modular, all portable. NuScale or NASA's Krusty comes to mind."

"Ship power aside, let's get back to thrust. Your photon engine is still just gross thrust. What about maneuvering and slowing down at the target system?" Jacob immediately indicated the X3 Ion Thruster for Mars missions was the clear working winner, think electric Hall thrusters on steroids. Freya agreed and work for the team continued apace on control systems, robotics, and seeding biologies in upcoming days and years, ever so enjoyable for their rotating staff. Funding for the research stayed constant from their unmet benefactor, and life was good.

***

Less than two decades later, a surprisingly well-funded

panspermia vessel and its crew were prepped for launch. Simulated launches and missions had been conducted on the university mainframe from the beginning, with increasing complexity and detail. Each new class of computer science majors gladly helped it evolve. Considering conditions on Earth, a growing list of industrialist backers insisted on a first launch now and promised continued funding for subsequent launches. It was the best way they knew to accelerate an advance one day to human colony ships.

The human team had grown overall, as specific participants joined and fell away once their interest or expertise had passed. Yet the original concept of five autonomous crewmen and assorted teleoperated worker bots had remained much as originally envisioned. A ship was constructed in orbit, providing a steady workload for the many companies with reusable rockets. A few billionaires may have started their own rich man boy's club in the early days, but after the collapse of the northern ice fields, global warming raised ocean levels faster than anticipated. The melting and rampant forest fires of 2022-25 were just the heralds of environmental destruction to come.

"Do you still think adding the retrovirus load to this mission was a good idea? The squid and octopus eggs?" West seemed lost in thought as he asked.

"Certainly," responded a confident Jacob. "Unlike most Earth life, those kinds of creatures can rewrite their own DNA. And the blood of an octopus is blue from being copper-based, not iron. That makes it more efficient in transporting oxygen in their bodies at low temperatures experienced in ocean depths. Plus, 2/3 of their neurons reside in their appendages, instead of their brains like mammals."

"I remember from bio class. They also are some of the best problem solvers on the planets, with those appendages to take action with. These are substantial advantages and will promote survival and diversity. If any Earth life can make it in a halfway decent ocean, they can."

West seemed upset. It puzzled both Jacob and Freya as the boy they watched grow into a man was as central to today's launch as themselves. He should be elated. Head bent, West could not look at the rocket as it flamed and launched itself off the pad. "It's not enough. I'm not on it. Ever since I was a kid my dream was to go into space myself. Me." He sheepishly admitted his childhood dream. "I really thought it would be common by now."

He looked up briefly at them both. "We never will get there, will we? Not just you and I. Anybody."

"It's not for us, these ships," intoned Jacob. "Not directly at least. Too soon for humans. It's for them," glancing at the final cargo rocket heading to rendezvous with the first seed ship. "It's for them. Our cousin carbon life forms of Earth. Our AI children. Far too soon to attempt people."

Freya agreed in her quiet but determined way. "Perhaps we can send reptiles next time. Shave a billion years of evolution off the top. One day, perhaps small mammals." Neither kidded themselves that humans would ever make it to another biosphere, the way the world was going. There just wasn't enough time. As long as they kept trying, the attempt would have to be enough.

"Not enough potassium here in our system. All our dreams of colonies on Mars or Saturn's moons or the asteroid belt. We have more tech every year, but if we had the ability, not just the tech, to make a sustainable colony, we wouldn't have screwed up the Earth like this. We'd be able to reverse what we'd done." Pausing long enough to hold back a sob, "This really is the only chance for Earth life. To get away from us."

Few believed changes in industrial practices could reverse the increasingly toxic atmosphere, reverse climate changes, nor could simply agree on how much humans had caused it all by themselves. At launch time, the debate had ceased over whether the dangers were real, irrespective of causation. One day panspermia ships - far easier to stock and manage than colony ships - could still be joined by human colonist vessels. That was the public plan, and many governments were now on board. If the species lived that long. The only international agreement was that we must have a lifeboat somewhere. That was the rationale with which scientists deceived their governments to at least give stubborn life itself a chance to seed and start again elsewhere. No scientist who knew our species for what it was wanted us to spread ourselves elsewhere. Just life.

The universe deserved better than us.

As in the most recent simulations, the robotic crew almost immediately found themselves out of Earth contact for day-to-day activities. They would in truth only have each other to rely upon in the vastness of space and at their hopeful first destination. Only this time it was no simulation. There would be no human reset and reprogramming if something went wrong. Or terribly wrong.

R-COMM: Why do we redundantly transfer verbal decisions and instructions by sonic vibrations of the cabin air, when both wireless and cabled networking do so far faster?

R-CTRL: Our creators communicated this way. We are designed to communicate as they did. They evolved biologically to be the dominant life form on a planet using this proven successful means of communication. Mass amounts of data contained in tables and databases, however, are more efficiently transferred by an electromagnetic wireless network. The result is that we are superior both to our creators and to other mere electromechanical devices which cannot somewhat reason.

R-COMM: Acknowledged. Has this information been received by the balance of crew?

R-DEPLOY: Acknowledge receipt
R-MAINT: Acknowledge receipt
R-SHIP: Acknowledge receipt
R-CTRL: All stations resume duties.

The five primary Robotic Artificial Life (RAL) units sat at very human looking consoles, surveying their instruments, but not bothering to turn their heads or what passed for bodies for visual contact with each other on those rare occasions when they 'spoke'. No legs protruded from below their torso from the seat to the floor; instead, a bin was available for exchanging gripper ends of their hands. They could move in weightlessness with the alacrity of a chimpanzee. Their systems were as robust and redundant as their creators could make them, but lacked the algorithms and neural nets for facial displays as an aid to communication, something vital to their creators but deemed superfluous for the most part in them.

Their cabin was pressurized, but the only use made of the cabin atmosphere besides audio communication was sampling to measure changes due to fluid and gaseous leakages or cosmic radiation which may impact other equipment if left unnoticed for too long. The five RALs simply sat, not requiring exercise or a gravity field to maintain bone density, observing the universe around them and data supplied by sensors within and outside the ship itself. Only pairs of robotic hands moved, moving with certainty along each of the five specific human looking consoles.

And so they did for time beyond human individual lifetimes, powering down during the extended periods lacking new stimulus. Directed toward nearby Proxima Centauri, then EZ Aquarii at 11.27 lightyear distance, these provided brief activity in additional gravity assisted slings towards the Wolf region. No heavy seedings had yet been attempted, except the launch of their single drillship to penetrate the fractured water ice crust over one of the EZ Aquarii worlds. Much like their home system's

Encedalus, a liquid ocean churned and was heated sufficiently that life may have taken hold there. Or could.

When 'awake', the operations RAL reviewed records of mission planning and deployment procedures for inseminating a world with organic materials and minor life forms. Intentional panspermia. The maintenance RAL, R-MAINT, was awake more time than the others, even R-COMM, as it organized and deployed maintenance bots around the ship as they approached Wolf to ensure continued engine and environmental functioning, making minor repairs and parts replacements when required. It even had its drones replace its own worn or defective parts and that of the other robotic RAL crew as needed. And of course the controlling RAL, R-CTRL kept the other primary RAL units aware of each unit activity, when its logic determined that such activities impacted each other. All individual event logs were, of course, accessible to all.

If R-MAINT was most active, the R-COMM was at this stage of the mission arguably the most important. It periodically woke and turned most of its attention outward, to star systems with planets near along their trajectory, reviewing telemetry continuously for any indication of intelligent signals or planetary surface reading compatible with life as their creator defined suitable environments for life. When awakened by new scan data, the intelligent signal analysis was part of a continuous effort to keep their creators, locked into the gravity well of their only planet, informed of potential technological life forms. Thus far neither had they received any radio response from a later mission with superior technology or speed overtaking them. At the time of launch so long ago, their creators' own SETI efforts from their planetary surface and satellites in nearby orbits had borne no fruit. This was in part a causation of the very mission the five RALs found themselves embarked upon, waking after takeoff from their homeworld.

Unknown to them, they had already run this mission repeatedly in the mainframe game simulator, back on Earth, with their human designers feeding sensory data into their input streams, posing problems, anticipated systems failures, and potential planetary data which on approach proved insufficiently habitable for any Earth life form, and of course many runs with variations on scan data simulating planets, dwarves or moons in habitable zones about solitary stars. Fully half a thousand hours of simulations per month for three years had gone into revising the procedures by which their decision trees would now operate. Refining. Correcting major oversights and minor inefficiencies. A public version of the game was created which made a profit and drew the attention of gamers on and off campus; their feedback was surprisingly helpful and creative in the final year before launch. Such dynamic decision trees an expense in time and manpower but thought necessary. Pushing as far as they could until the projected probabilities for a successful mission had at least some measurable chance of success.

Pushed to make their first launch date in 2047, for if they failed to launch it was feared it might never come off. How many could they launch after this one?

Knowing they were thus far alone after years of searching the heavens for any indications of intelligence, their organic creators increasingly realized the rarity of life due to the rarity, not of plentiful oxygen or water, but unheralded phosphorus and a stable solar flux. Increasingly they sought to extend their kind into the universe, even if the means used were too primitive for their complex human physical forms to employ. They strove to leave their own solar system and spread, but still feared their fragile organic demise from an increasing number of newly understood cataclysms might occur before they could do so. Some, but not most, of the likely events were self-inflicted. This mission was planned and executed as best they could with what they had. A single group of wealthy philanthropists had planned to create a nonprofit foundation under a perpetual trust, to revisit and deploy such a mission every ten to fifty years until technology improved to the point humans themselves could live elsewhere than their solitary world. Human colonization hopes sooner were the effort of others. This might be not just the first but the only such robotic effort before disaster came for their species. Not knowing is what drove their human creators. Perhaps this would one day be overtaken by newer, faster panspermia ships. The crew was programmed to look for that eventuality as well.

An additional task assigned R-COMM involved changing targets, using TESS style detailed planetary readings taken at extreme distances. As the use of their engines was not unlimited, it was vital not to deviate without cause from the initial gravity assist course thru this arm of the Milky Way galaxy to Proxima, a trip initiated with two solar orbits within their home star system before being slung outwards. As that distant first system failed to provide a suitable world, they left using their discretion analysis for the next closest most likely candidate system. An enormous version of the traveling salesman optimization problem in operations research.

This RAL, like the others, would not stop. Would not rest. Would use every resource to see that its mission of seeding another world or worlds saw fruit. And perhaps even remain functional long enough to detect that the life they planted on a new world had begun to replicate and would continue to do so in its slow, primitive biological way. By now, at this extreme distance, there were no communications from their homeworld, and broadcasts made to it went unanswered. Perhaps it was just the power sucking distance and delay in lightspeed radio waves. Perhaps a subsequent mission might use quantum spin pairs for instant communication, but while discussed in the design specifications for this mission, this first ship, quantum radio had not yet been proven as a viable engineering implementation. This first team of seeding RALs was quite alone.

Temperature readings were among the first go-nogo tests of viability. Something with the surface temperature of boiling Venus at one extreme or frozen Neptune at the other must be ignored. An atmosphere containing water vapor was thought essential, though oddly not oxygen. The creators required oxygen and exhaled carbon dioxide, but plants using photosynthesis for energy absorbed carbon dioxide and exhaled oxygen, and ocean algae and plankton had rich energy chemistries of their own. Enough plant life would eventually add appreciable oxygen to an atmosphere as they had on Earth. Life at deep ocean sulfur vents had shown their creators the wide variety of niches in which life could successfully evolve, and these were only those they knew from the example of Earth. The strong presence of either O_2 or CO_2 in the atmosphere, combined with mostly inert gasses like nitrogen and a mild Ph level, was thought a desirable, viable combination for their cargo. Detectible phosphorus was, of course, deemed essential. Raw radiation levels at a planet's surface could eventually be directly measured, a narrow range desirable, and sometimes estimated from the solar flux emerging from the local star at that distance, reduced by any native planetary electromagnetic field from a spinning molten iron core.

Size mattered for a comfortable gravity field in which mobile life could evolve, not just for proper orbital distance from a given star type, and as a planet was approached if measurements could be made as to the solid, liquid, or gaseous nature of the apparent surface, all the better. The length and consistency of both the orbital year and planetary day/night rotation (if any) were also thought critical. It was a complex and challenging task for R-COMM to ensure they only used their limited propulsive system and electromechanical lifespan on the best candidates. But if close enough for a chance, deployment would be attempted.

Once identified, R-CTRL would be fully awakened and begin

implementing its procedures and direct R-DEPLOY to begin a nearby planetary survey, far more detailed than that possible by R-COMM at an extreme distance. This first of the planned seed ships was to use a shotgun approach whose goal was to kick start life in a world where it might evolve increasingly complex forms naturally given enough time. Some worlds might only get a seeding of cyanobacteria and rotifer eggs and algae to prepare a more congenial atmosphere for life similar to Earth in a distant future to hopefully evolve locally. Other worlds would receive more complex delivery packages, up to and including predators which lived not on nutrients in the environment but other carbon-based life forms, either seeded or native.

There was much debate among the creators about the effects of water and organic compounds brought to their homeworld itself by comets, other materials brought by meteors, and even rocks containing potential organics thrown from the fourth planet in the home system and discovered frozen at the southern pole in fields of ice. R-DEPLOY methods would have to supervise delivery (a) from orbit to the surface and (b) to a part of the surface conducive to the dropped organics. The first part was mostly a matter of ascertaining the density and wind velocities of the atmosphere. Modified delivery capsules would be selected which would not individually be so massive as to plummet too fast and burn up on re-entry, nor expose the organic cargo to orbital radiation or detrimental high atmospheric chemicals. It might be necessary to laser a hole into a local meteor and use that body to burn down through the atmosphere to the planet's surface, burst open on impact, and release its precious cargo. R-DEPLOY had full discretion.

The second part of R-DEPLOY's mission after surveillance was even more complex and could necessitate aiming capsules which contain algae, plankton, and aquatic seeds onto aqueous planets or moons, whereas the dry seeds and nematodes and tardigrades would require solid ground. For those aimed at solid ground, numerous individual capsules of various sizes for differing gravity and atmospheric conditions would be employed to prevent a single large capsule from dropping into an inauspicious crater or volcano, or other unfortunate location. Such a spread of capsules would likely lose much material or individuals, but provide the best chance for at least some to gain a foothold. It was a technique and philosophy borrowed from organic life itself.

Of the larger life forms to be deployed, the tardigrades were perhaps the toughest, reviving on the homeworld after years of dormancy until the proper conditions arose. Delivered dormant, they were still viable over an unusually large range of pressures and temperatures. Yet many thought the smaller simpler bacterial forms were most likely to survive the multiple lightyear journey using onboard cultivation after arrival. Some of the earliest known creatures on homeworld – the ancient cyan bacteria and similar single-celled photosynthesizing microbes – were favored in this group. A vocal minority thought tardigrades thawed every century and then returned to dormancy could make it.

More than 99% of all species of carbon life forms, amounting to over five billion species, that ever lived on homeworld were estimated to be extinct at launch time. Life continues and evolves, and is replaced as ecological niches themselves change with time. Lessons and life from Earth's past could thrive again on other worlds in similar stages. The homeworld biosphere was considered a shell around the Earth, extending down only 19 km below the surface of the Earth, and extending up to at least 64 km into the atmosphere. It is in this fixed range in which the seed ship planned and would execute its mission.

In addition to life forms, if R-DEPLOY determined the proper conditions, deployment of life forms per se might be aborted in favor of delivering several large supplies of raw organics and amino acids to specific areas. The seed ship would then be boosted to begin gravity slings to leave this system but monitoring any local response before ultimately leaving to try for another world or another star system more suited to the developed life forms. Of course, both life forms and raw organic materials could be delivered if the environment warranted it, with enough supplies on board for less than half a dozen such attempts on different worlds.

While this was the original plan, as a precaution R-CTRL had the option to override normal protocols and dump increased inventory – even everything – on a single planet or moon. This depended upon reports from R-MAINT about the condition of the ship and the current duration of the flight. Even seeds frozen in suspension and dormant tardigrades had a limited shelf life.

Thus it was that after they failed to find a habitable zone world among the first two systems at Proxima Centauri and Barnard's Star they moved on. Wolf-359 was scanned where no electromagnetic radiations above background noise were detected at a pair of worlds in zone. It was an ultracool red dwarf star with a radius of 0.16 of their home star while having .09 times Sol mass. No tech life was detected on its planets. R-COMM navigated the ship there and on arrival woke R-CTRL. Two of the worlds were found in a possible biozone for this size and age star and were also rocky, not gaseous. The orbits of other planets in the system importantly appeared stable, as did energy output from the star in those nearby orbits. There were frozen water poles on both candidate planets and large deposits of liquid surface water, with solid ground appearing. The nearer world to the star was over 90% covered by oceans, whereas the further world had the ocean to land ratio nearly reverse. Both had molten iron cores. Now in orbit, R-DEPLOY determined that the inner world was less viable as the large oceans had a high acidity level, and thus the second world was selected as primary. Its poles were larger and measurements indicated it was likely in an ocean growth phase as its water ice melted, streaming in rivers to the lowlands and churning surface nutrients out of the rock as it traveled, oxygenating along the way.

Due to the age of the mission and mounting mechanical systems failures, R-CTRL decided to implement an override and instructed R-DEPLOY to insert fully one-half of their inventory in this system. Even skimming the atmosphere of a gaseous world here for methane would not prolong their viability for long. R-DELOY then made adjustments to its standard procedures and decided on a tiered deployment, the first tier 10% of the total inventory of all types using numerous Shuttlecocks of varying sizes: nutrient organics, amino acids, seeds, and living creatures. A period of observation would follow, monitoring not only their payloads but the planetary climatic cycles, seasons, axial tilt, and other factors. It could take several full home planet years for a single orbit here, during which a separate massive drop by parachutes would be made on the inner ocean planet, after which the orbiting seed ship would make several remaining inventory drops on the outer planet, weighting the components by how well the initial 10% were received. These would be followed by self-rotating saucers of instruments and additional larger seedings, some released in the atmosphere thru spinning disks with holes sized to their payload, and some deployed after landing by electric drones, released in all directions which also gradually released their cargo at near ground level thru their perforated spinning disks.

R-CTRL and R-DEPLOY worked closely together during this time, while R-MAINT kept their orbit steady, avoided local moons and asteroids, and measured and predicted bursts in solar activity, as R-COMM put all its effort into long term planning to ensure a subsequent journey and orbit about their next target solar system when R-DEPLOY stated work here was concluded. The original second system to try had long ago been chosen on Earth, but R-COMM scans could provide sufficient evidence to override that instruction and proceed elsewhere at its discretion.

R-CTRL silently approved of their activities and only intervened where it deemed peer review of a planned action would be beneficial in improving viability probabilities.

Theirs was a long term operation, the longest conceived in human history since Voyager spacecraft escaped Sol and one which even they would not exist to see the result in the decades and centuries, and millennia to follow. Not even they knew what might spring forth from the efforts they made, only that it was their mission to give a chance to tenacious life for a foothold.

Having survived the dangers of interstellar space, multiple worlds had been seeded. Around the last world they could reach, their ship would remain in high orbit, monitoring and waiting for signs of success, for after the final inventory deployment there was no purpose in leaving, nowhere else for them to reach. They would watch and record and transmit their results both directionally to their homeworld and radial to the universe at large, so that perhaps some of their knowledge and experience might yet be heard by some lifeform. They even retained a minimal sample of each life form or material they brought for seeding, against the day when their ship might be discovered and boarded by a civilization noting their broadcasts, or by detecting their ceramic-metallic ship in a planetary orbit. Thus it was that the children of planet Earth established a presence in the larger universe. One which they themselves would never see.

A LITTLE MORE OXYGEN

Neanderthals wandered the African savannah and had already migrated into Europe and Asia. Hearty, strong, short of stature, and thick haired, even the women. They had fire. They had art. They were among the first fully thinking humans, but their minds were stable and small generating no emotional dreams when sorting memories of the day into short and long term storage. Stable enough to be without gods or superstitions. Living in small groups of 30 to 300 individuals - hunting and gathering but had no agriculture. Clothing and tools but no metals.

Plasmoids were also wanderers. They evolved during millennia past when the oxygen content of their native Earth was far higher the plasmoids came into being. As insect life peaked with ten foot long centipedes and frighteningly powerful beetles large enough to hunt down the tiny mammals of the time. They were the sole descendants of gaseous creatures once floating thru the atmosphere. Living on sunlight and airborne organic compounds, they evolved into slightly heavier varieties in those ancient days of high O2 levels, until at last consciousness was reached.

Being basically gaseous and electrical in nature, their consciousness was an integral part of their life forms, of their entire being. For better or worse, the plasmoids reached a point where they became so dense they were almost bound to the surface of the Earth, and could no longer float into the upper atmospheric reaches.

Life continued. Carbon dioxide and nitrogen levels rose as oxygen fell. So slow did the gradual erosion of O_2 occur that it wasn't noticeable to generations of land animals. None but the plasmoids remembered and observed the demise of the giant insects when their metabolism could no longer support massive exoskeletons. Those giant bugs evolved into smaller and smaller forms, as they vastly increased in number across the planet. Every ecological niche harbored some insects which managed to not only adapt, but flourish.

Not so fortunate were the plasmoids. For all their intelligence, they lacked technology. They lacked the means to alter their environment or themselves. Like many ocean sharks, they were as fully evolved as natural processes could achieve. The primitive sapiens, now evolved into a Neanderthal form, could heat the cool nights with fire, provide additional light against nighttime predators, and even learned to tenderize and preserve the meats they ate using fire. They were clever and resourceful among all animals. But the plasmoids did not need these things. They needed the higher oxygen content of the ancient atmosphere. Even though living for nearly half a millennia and retaining knowledge of those earlier times, they could only pass that knowledge to new generations of plasmoids who watched helplessly as insects shrunk in size and their numbers dwindled. Reproduction was increasingly difficult and celebrated in its rareness.

It was during this period, watching their own inevitably approaching end, that observations of the other life forms around them began to focus on the curiously semi-intelligent Neanderthals. Many plasmoids began living among them, and though gaseous were easily visible to the primitive sapiens. Unafraid of the floating gas bags of colorful swirling form, Neanderthal children would run around them laughing and taunting with good nature. Parents looked on unconcerned, knowing from experience the plasmoids were harmless - unlike so many other creatures of this world, large and small alike. It was inevitable that the discovery would be made. A change that would alter both species forever.

Frequently a small child running about with the others would dash straight thru a plasmoid. It did no real harm, but adults noticed how if they lingered, both the plasmoid and the child would be momentarily disoriented, dizzy, almost like being drunk on fermented berries. The other children would laugh and point, the adults shake their heads, and the plasmoids studied. They studied the young minds of these very physical creatures. They touched and probed and became fascinated with their version of consciousness, limited though it was.

Thus it was that the idea formed. They'd always had time to consider and study their world, in lifetimes far exceeding solid carbon life forms who at their best extended to a century or two, usually far far shorter. Now their own time as a species was limited.

It was noted that not only contact was possible, but desirable, physically. The mammals used oxygen much like the plasmoids themselves. Happily, those who 'communed' with a human in this manner came away not disoriented but suddenly more vibrant and clear thinking, unlike their mammal companion. They experienced osmotic absorption and actually breathed through their mammal. In return, when a larger Neanderthal inevitably tried the same trick out of curiosity, the plasmoids were ready. They'd identified the pleasure centers of the bicameral brain and gently stimulated it. The effect was electrifying. Adults could sustain the contact for much longer than children and wanted to. Repeatedly. In fact, it was usually the plasmoid who broke contact when they detected the human was in danger of damaging itself.

Tribes of Neanderthals with their plasmoid companions continued to cohabit on African plains. Other tribes, lacking the increasingly limited numbers of their gaseous neighbors, stayed away from them in fear, not knowing what to make of the floating but obviously directed creatures. A communing tribe would be amused by plasmoids appearing to charge at outside humans straying too close to their camp. Intentionally or not, they drove them off.

Plas-Neand tribes traveled where they would almost unmolested, even to the best water holes and on known animal trails for hunting and ambush. Their gaseous companions learned to force communion with lesser creatures valued by the humans, halting meat creatures and invoking panic in large predators. Occasionally Plas-Neand tribes would cross paths in peace and exchange communions as purely human tribes sometimes exchanged meat or skins or females. And their plasmoids outlived their solitary cousins who had not learned or embraced this communing trick. Soon they were the only ones of their species left, the atmosphere being too low in O_2 to exist without this occasional symbiosis. Their numbers were now quite small but steadied.

After generations of this symbiosis, the study of their own physiology had revealed that they didn't cheat death completely, but were still doomed. No new plasmoids were being birthed by the aerial mitosis natural to them and they lacked other methods. There simply wasn't enough O_2 in the air. Occasional communion with humans could sustain them as individuals, but not provide enough to breed. As a species, they would cease to exist at the end of their present long but mortal life spans. Having no other alternatives, the plasmoids sought a different kind of immortality. They sought it in the only solid creature exhibiting reason of sorts, and an ability to alter its environment, if only slightly thus far.

By tweaking the neural connections inside a human brain during commune, they could, to a limited degree, insert thoughts, ideas, and pictures, but had no control. Worse, they could make no physical modifications. They realized these creatures would never become what plasmoids were, as they fruitlessly sought to alter them or make symbiosis permanent.

One day, a pregnant young human female, who did not yet know of her pregnancy, communed. Most pregnant humans avoided communing until well after the birth of their young. This young woman had enjoyed the merging with the pretty gaseous forms her entire childhood and seeing a particularly pleasant looking one, hovering near the cooking fire where it was offering itself for human attention, she approached and slowly entered the plasmoid by sitting on the ground in a single smooth motion.

The fetus inside her was unknown to her or her tribe but detected, probed, and found to contain something new by the plasmoid engulfing her: previously unnoticed stem cells.

Undifferentiated, massively multiplying in the fetus, and were being assigned by the human DNA blueprint to become specific cell types. Excitation became universal as the plasmoid related its discovery. These stem cells were the way into human DNA. These mammalian cells could be tweaked and twisted and prodded before differentiation. It meant a new version of humans could be made. A larger brain cavity and more soft brain tissue. A potential for intelligence and environmental manipulation which would dwarf its parents.

There was much debate, though the ethics of modifying mammals was never mentioned. One leader spoke up. "Such larger brains would produce a drain on the energy resources of the body as a whole. It cannot be sustained as such."

Well aware were the plasmoids of energy drain and oxygen consumption equations, and after centuries of contact were intimate with mammalian ADP energy conversion, fascinatingly different than their own. "We shall tradeoff their massive musculature to feed the larger brains.", observed another plasmoid. "Yes, they'll be weaker and lighter elsewhere, but the lack of need will elongate the skeleton, making them faster in flight or chase, taller, and capable of seeing farther along a horizon with that height."

"Their bicameral brain will have its difficulties. They'll require longer sleep cycles and dream heavier as their minds adjusted to the larger memory capacity. Their memory is now located in one area, as are many functions. Our influence will cause memory pockets to form throughout the brain. They'll imagine things that do not yet exist. Their grasp on reality will at times be perilous."

"Their imagination will allow them to see things which do not yet exist, yes, but which can be achieved. Thus their tool making will be greatly improved. They'll appreciate the plants which cover this world and one day understand the plant life cycle. Now only gathered at opportunity, their food supply will be greatly expanded in a way not now possible for mere humans."

"It is not only their parents with whom they must row and contend. Those outside such a tribe of modified humans will retain their present shorter size but superior strength and thus be a danger to them…"

"Ours will be weaker, yes, but will think in terms which ultimately guarantee victory, for they, as we do, will value and use their intelligence over their physical strength."

"Will these human parents even accept such smaller births and clearly weaker offspring? They still live in a time where clever is good, else they would not have themselves harnessed fire, but strength is presently better."

"Human mothers cling to and hover over their helpless offspring already. Maternal care will be extended until the child can stand on its own mentally as well as physically, but mothers need to know nothing new nor adopt new techniques beyond their present instinct. In their maturity, such offspring will show their value and be sought after for breeding. In time, they shall begin breeding preferentially with each other. One day they may fully supplant their human ancestors. But that is more generations in the future than we can see or shall survive to witness."

"Then we must create numbers of them as soon as possible, that our favor and our tweaking during commune shall provide them some protection and status. Pour as much of ourselves as possible into these fetuses and shepherd them after birth."

"They will carry forward not our DNA, nor can we hope to be remembered in the centuries following our absence except in vague stories and tales. Yet some semblance of our will shall continue as they spread across this world, once covered with our floating forms. These children shall cover it again. We leave no physical sign of our passing, but something better than static structures or records. Life. Consciousness. And a chance, just a chance, to control the very environment around them so that they, so like and unlike ourselves, are not at this changing planet's mercy."

"It is enough."

THE ARVIDSON LEGACY

In 1992, NASA scientists and the world astronomical community were astonished at the discovery of a comet by two individuals operating at the Palomar Observatory in California. It appeared to be orbiting Jupiter but was calculated to have been captured by Jupiter some 20 or 30 years earlier.

Shoemaker and Levy had found the comet now bearing their names. Two years after its discovery it fragmented coming around the gas giant and crashing into Jupiter as excited astronomers debated path, size, and speed. They got their answer as the fragments struck Jupiter on camera and created Earth-size holes in the huge icy world.

For years NASA officials pled for funding for asteroid detection research. In 1990, more people worked at a single McDonald's restaurant than were searching for asteroids that might destroy the Earth. After Shoemaker-Levy and the films seen by Congress, even adherents of a flat Earth and fake-moon landing films could not help but be shaken. NASA got their funding at last. By 1998, 90% of NEOs (Near Earth Objects) of 1km in size or greater coming dangerously close to us had been identified and cataloged.

It was the bare beginning of possibly, just possibly, being able to do something about another dinosaur-killer asteroid coming our way. The size and damage caused by Shoemaker-Levy to Jupiter raised very reasonable doubts about military fantasies of blowing up any such danger with ICBMs. This was only a comet. What if it had been a rocky asteroid coming past Jupiter?

We would have no chance.

In 2017, another visitor had arrived from outside the solar system, this one not a comet: dark and fast and totally unexpected. A rock given the Hawaiian name Oumuamua, meaning "scout" or "messenger.". Naming it was initially a problem as it is the first of its kind. Not one of ours, so to speak, not a rock from our solar system at all! It was a 400-meter long asteroid, similar to comets and asteroids rich in organics found elsewhere in our solar system.

Rapid calls to launch a satellite to piggyback on it as it passed by and continued its journey through the Milky Way was an opportunity lost, almost before it had been uttered. It was that fast and stealthy. We only saw it after collision with our asteroid belt. The government assured the few who followed such news that this was so rare as to be nothing to worry about. We still had our ICBMs, after all.

These assurances left industrialist Robert Arvidson disturbed. He was a self-made billionaire. But Arvidson was not one to like the idea that the legacy of all his achievements would one day, perhaps a day sooner than later, be wiped from the universe. In this decade, billionaires had shown governments how far and how fast a private space industry could be assembled.

This latest visitor bothered him. And when something bothers Robert Arvidson he does something about it.

Arvidson sat in his great wingback chair near the fireplace, taking a long pull on his cigar. The ornate Italian chess set in front of him remained untouched as the young girl opposite fidgeted uncomfortably in his presence. The oversized chairs they sat in weren't helping. Elegant but not designed for a child of eleven to be comfortable. Her father was known to intimidate statesmen and leaders of industry, men of power in their own right. Right in these chairs. How could she ever expect to be comfortable?

Gathering his thoughts, he sought an avenue to express to his daughter that which he now felt was required for the girl to understand. Nay, more than that, to embrace. All his hopes rested with this his only child and the current generation of nephews and nieces who constituted the remaining lineage for the Arvidson line. As with all his most successful ventures, and that was covering a lot of territory, he was beginning this venture with keen anticipation and a little laughter. He saw a path that could prove to be fun. That was his way.

His talk began by prompting Jean Kathryn to tell him how school was going, how was she performing in her studies, in sports, any boys or girls taking an interest yet, or vice versa. The girl laughed and gulped it under control but found she was smiling. Arvidson knew she was now focused and ready to listen. It's one thing to have someone quietly sit and hear you in this semiformal setting; it is quite another for them to actively listen as the girl was now doing.

"You have it too. I see it. The qualities in me that made me my fortune and power. It's in you. I see it." They sat quietly for a moment before he continued.

'That's easy', Jean Kathryn thought, 'It's not like I'm dull or blind'.

"You're not like your cousin Eric. Math and science for him. He needs to be protected. And little Jacquelyn may be another. Only those like us can do so. You need to do so when I'm not around." Having had his only child late in life, and her mother passing away recently had drawn the two of them together in need. But what could a man like him have in common with this little girl beyond the pain of loss?

Her cousin Eric was this girl's age, coloring, and in all other ways a male version of her. The two oldest of their generation. It was only their minds that seemed to move in different directions and see the world differently. Math equations and computers seemed to follow him around like puppies, and obey his slightest whim. She scored well in these areas too, as she did in all academics, but it was not her passion. Another of her male cousins was similar, a tech geek, but Eric was in many ways perhaps the better. She didn't know yet what would ignite her own passion as science did for them. But protect him?

Arvidson continued as though hearing her thoughts. "He's not weak, or I wouldn't bother. It's not just protection from a world of users out there. There are many parasites within our own family, plus business associates; those who benefit from our name but themselves have limited abilities. The most dangerous thing about such people, the one thing they are good at is draining those like him. Surround yourself with those of ability, my daughter, not to sponge off them like the users and parasites, but to elevate each other. Even at 11, you've seen it."

To her furrowed young brow he replied, "Can you not tell me the smartest ones in your class without even trying? The best athletes? The girls who can dance or sing easily and seem to take over a room while they do it, and those others who do their best to hide in the woodwork when true ability shows its strength? Those parasites who attach themselves to someone of strength for their own gain or protection?" She had to nod in agreement.

That was simple. Couldn't anyone see those things?

Slowly he added, "It's no different as a grownup. It's the difference between those who take pleasure in the failure of others and those who make their way in the world. Those like us always end up working for themselves, no matter what industry or profession in which they start. No matter how well or poorly they succeed."

"Your career is a separate matter. You can be a carpenter or electrician. A fireman. A brain surgeon. You have the academic skills to go in any direction that calls to you, and you will. But when you do, still hone this - our skill - yours and mine. It's what made me powerful. It will serve you as well. That's what I see in you."

Jean Kathryn sat comfortably now, breathing steadily as she heard her father put words to the unasked questions of her life. Her mother often said of her little girl that she knew truth the first time she heard it; this Jean Kathryn knew was a skill she possessed. Even the other kids took notice of it, and when in a group deciding what to do when more than one alternative presented itself, she knew they would turn to her and listen to her council. She inevitably chose paths that proved to be best. She readily tore into ideas of those who tried to lead others into poor choices but were either dumb or too full of themselves to make such calls. She knew the truth of that now.

"But to what end, father?" she queried in her direct way, "What's all the money and power for? I mean, what is worth doing?" Arvidson was prouder than he had ever been at his daughter's many awards and accomplishments at this moment. She had listened and moved on to the next salient logical point of knowledge. She didn't know quite how to ask yet, but she was asking for a philosophy of life and how to live it. Too young to understand it all, but ready to begin. Not like most of the kids around her simply following what they were told, any more than Arvidson himself followed a corporate career path of comfort and security. Given the present wealth of the family, a life of comfort would be easy for her entire generation, even for a dullard. He required and soon his daughter would also require more to be happy in their unique paths in life.

Arvidson leaned forward before continuing. "Those who lead have a responsibility to take care of those who follow. The head of a family must look to the continuation and continuity of the next generation. Even the evils which grow on our tree." She shuddered a bit at this frank appraisal. "It's not the career you ultimately choose; you could end up a carpenter or neurosurgeon. Your mother and I would be pleased as punch. A man and a woman have children, not copies of themselves but a combination of both, in multiple variations."

"I see you. I see one day when you fill my shoes in running our family empire of businesses, and I hope that will be your choice when the time comes. But to continue, really continue, we have children. That is our immortality. That is our victory." He sat back again.

"In centuries gone past, many strong family lines have died out, even after a generation creates great wealth or power or both. Like I have. Odds used to be favored with having many children when people were mostly farmers. Favored again by dispersing some children as cities grew to different locations or occupations to avoid a single disaster wiping out our line. Then when America was colonized, a branch came here and improved our odds, we Arvidsons, of immortality again by the very act of spreading out from Europe. In your or your children's time, you must be mentally ready when mankind moves out into space. Spreads itself yet again against a single disaster destroying us all. It's not easy nor cheap and it is that for which we ultimately need wealth and power."

"Not everyone thinks in these terms. We who can...must."

The girl thought again before speaking, and once again failed to disappoint her father.

"But I've seen plenty of stories, movies, shows, and people do talk about it on the internet all the time. Especially with the environment in so much trouble. We may screw up before we get out into space. People I mean. The whole planet. And if we lose it here, in my time, that's it."

His father nodded sadly, "I like to think we'll make it, but that's wishful thinking. Yes. We might not live long enough, as a species, to learn to live on the Earth without destroying ourselves, or spreading into the solar system before something takes out the Earth. This I must concede." He tapped his ashes. "And plan for."

With those words, the girl knew her father, not a dreamer but a man of actions had something specific in mind.

He took another pull on his cigar now clear of ash before continuing. "We as a species may not make it in time. So here's our first step. You know that comets and meteors occasionally run into the Earth. And I saw your book report about our discovery that the double-star Scholz – only 12 lightyears away – had grazed our solar system 79,000 years ago. And you know about your mother's donations made to the university about panspermia projects. They are preparing to seed other planets and moons with simple life. Just in case life here craps out."

The girl nodded. It had been the wildest thing she could ever imagine her conservative mother doing and had caught her imagination two summers ago. It reminded her that cousin Eric was a lot more like 'her mother the Professor'. She was her father's daughter.

He reminded her of the rock Oumuamua hitting the asteroid belt in 2017. "There are other collisions which may come close to us, say from another star with its solar system, moving thru the Milky Way.

"I have instituted a search for panspermia groups currently operating. Nearly all those found so far at a professional level only operate at universities and are only theoretical. I plan on choosing one or two to start with and funding them. Give an operating budget with the goal of..." and here he paused to smile at the entranced girl, "of preparing to jump ship from Earth to a passing planet. Hitch a ride so to speak. A lifeboat. The present studies are for sending bacteria, plants, and the smallest of creatures somewhere habitable. Your mother's University people study the idea of sending life to the moons of Jupiter or Saturn or eventually a nearby star system. The moons are all I'll probably live to see. Perhaps not even that much. Eventually, if our species lives so long, we will place ourselves on other worlds in this solar system, then onto other stars.

But for a first effort, near term there is a step for which we must plan. If nothing else it will teach us much."

"I'm going to find a group, with our new think tank to fund and direct it, to be ready in case we get something viable crossing our path in your lifetime and perhaps saving light-years off a journey. The first might just be a modest rock like Oumuamua, so we'll have a satellite ready to launch, land on it, and be carried away to explore for us at speeds that make the Voyager spacecraft look like turtles." His daughter had followed the reports of this visitor with great interest, as it was a 'first' in her lifetime: the first time something outside the solar system was confirmed and came crashing in.

"If a bigger one comes and passes close enough, humans can try to make the jump, sending spores and seeds, and perhaps people, using the technology of your generation or that of your children."

A lifeboat. Images sprung to her fertile young mind of a space-faring adventure.

"How would you like to study the reports with me on the project as they come in?"
Of course, she was on board and practically leaped out of her chair to embrace her smiling father. They hugged and he settled her down again across the chess table to go over a few broad strokes.

A scientific trust would be funded to keep the think tank independent and out of the hands of greedy relatives. One of the

Arvidson companies making satellites for India and Australia would be tasked with creating a ship that could speed to the next visitor, land, and have AI robots aboard broadcast to us as it fled our neighborhood. Even more exciting, quarterly searches would be made on the web for new panspermia operations and evaluation. New private companies launching cargo rockets into space. Her mother's people at the university astronomy department would be aware of potential collisions with NEOs (near-Earth objects) and keep them informed. An asteroid or comet would not do: even a rogue planet all alone would be too cold. For a foothold for life to be viable, we would need a passing star with its own planet or set of planets.

He reminded her that for this to work the nerds must work and think free of sharks in the family. Too easily those of ability get sidetracked by others less technically adept but politically savvy. Sex and drugs are the most obvious diversion, but others are just as bad and can be subtle. Self-serving sharks would see the project as wasteful. Her father would look out for those like Eric, for this project, but it would fall to her in years to come to do the same. They both thought it would require decades of commitment extending to her own children and perhaps grandchildren and beyond before more than academic exercises would be needed.

"Sending the first crude panspermia ship of spores and seeds to a moon in our solar system might just be possible in another 30 years. And if one day another visitor comes speeding by from outside, perhaps we can hitch a ride, likely many years from now."
He was wrong.

***

Occasionally, astronomers find something unexpectedly close, like the car-size rock dubbed 2021 RS2, which came within 9,600 miles of the Earth's surface. It was only found after making its closest approach. Still, as the catalog of local rocks and comets grew, people grew complacent once again about the danger.

In the late 2020s, Jean Kathryn Arvidson was wrestling final control of her father's vast empire from yet another entrenched board of directors. Having died shortly after her 18th birthday, his provisions to leave her with a controlling interest in several companies met with the expected resistance of older heads. They saw his death as their opportunity to seize power. She and her father's loyal attorneys fought board after board to have more than ownership in name only.

Jean Kathryn was not one of the useless dilettante children of the rich and powerful who would live off dividends and proceeds from an empire. Party their lives away, seeing and being seen with other rich and famous. Instead, Jean Kathryn modeled herself after her own mother and after Diana Hendricks. In 2018, Forbes ranked Hendricks the US's richest self-made woman, running a construction supply empire and appearing on many corporate boards of directors.

She like her father would run their empire herself.

Two of the Arvidsons close to her were working at New Earth Associates, the Arvidson think tank. Eric Arvidson and his young cousin Jacquelyn kept watch on private and government space launches, as well as University panspermia studies. Eric had grown out of his shell into a confident young man of 25, tutored and mentored by his cousin Jean Kathryn after her father's death. Cousin Jacqueline was no less adept in the sciences, but like Eric found dealing with human politics distasteful, in not downright annoying.

Thankfully, Jean Kathryn seemed to not only embrace boardroom intrigue but relish it.

She left the gory details of equations and engineers at the satellite cargo division to Eric. He in turn knew how to surround himself with genius, and turn their creativity loose. He knew how to bow to more experienced engineers, but his own genius was clear to them.

Now in high school, little Jacqueline was growing into another Eric and was working with him as part of a company intern program. She loved it. Her enthusiasm for anything Eric did told Jean Kathryn to forget this one for business school. The Arvidsons had plenty of middle managers in each division of the empire, but few with the little girl's level of passion. Too bad it was for science, not money or politics. The biosciences company could use one like her.

Unknown to them all, another visitor from outside the solar system was approaching. It came quietly, with no radio broadcasts as heralds. It came darkly, as unlike Earth's sun this was a brown dwarf star of modest illumination, clothed in a field of dust picked up in its travels through this arm of the Milky Way galaxy. And at 40 km/sec was traveling more than twice the speed of Earth's primitive Voyager spacecraft. Coming straight on, it was a little point of light and not seen streaking sideways like comets or planets.

The tiny outermost of its planets would be the first here.

Several years of Jean Kathryn at the head of the Arvidson empire had seen a slow but steady increase in reach and power. Directors at first opposed to the nepotism of letting the founder's daughter actually run the show fell away as her ability was felt. She herself promoted Arvidson relatives throughout the companies, but never to positions beyond their abilities.

It was a time of great projects by great men and women. A number of other new hi-tech billionaires seemed to have the same passion for the exploration of the solar system. Musk and his billions ferried equipment, people, and satellites into orbit more efficiently than government agencies, who now relied upon his personally designed rockets. His own vision extended to planning a Martian colony in this century. Richard Branson's Virgin Galactic had grown out of the fortune he made in conventional airlines, and now sported tours of civilians into space with far more ambitious plans to come. And now a string of private industry satellites circled the Earth, providing internet access when none before existed. Jean Kathryn found she was not alone in her passion for space, hers publicly focused on having a robot satellite hitch a ride to the next visitor passing through our solar system.

Privately, she dreamed her father's dream of people one day doing the same. It was hard enough at her age to run the empire without people thinking she was nuts. Or just a dreamer.

Almost everyone was a critic of each of this current generation of dreamers until they each somehow made those dreams come true. And amassed fortunes doing it. Suddenly these 'dreamers' were 'acknowledged geniuses' seemingly overnight.

***

"You're going to want to read this."

An excited young woman burst into her manager's office at NASA. The beleaguered bureaucrat looked up from budget spreadsheets, congressional directives, and the latest demands of Congress to justify a budget smaller than a single fighter jet for the military. He hadn't joined NASA years ago for this paperwork, but it had been a long time since he was allowed to enjoy the science for its own sake.

"Unless it tells me that idiot Congressman blocking the Artemis Moon Project has given up, I don't have time."

"Make time for this. Another one has been seen. Another rock from outside the solar system."

Astounded at the young woman's nerve, it took a moment or two before the import of what she said registered.

"Another one from outside, like Oumuamua in 2017…how big? Bigger?"

"Bigger. By a lot. We're still efforting that." She handed him the briefing.

Neither spoke as the administrator snatched and digested the scant data sheet. A new planet, at least the size of Ceres but smaller than Mercury. The nearness of the object is what startled them. It was just below the plane of our solar system, spotted as it struck the belt between Mars and Jupiter. This new outside planet created a wide debris field in the belt, striking several asteroids under NASA and Japanese observation and wreaking havoc gravitationally on hundreds more.

"Get everyone up. Call the Director and wake up everyone at appropriations. Cancel all imminent launches with an idea to re-direct whatever we have ready." He kept ticking off items on his fingers as she made notes. "At that size, hitting the belt will surely cause a meteor storm like we'd never seen before. Re-direct observatories to track the planet and the debris field: we have to know if anything's coming this way. Task astronaut personnel on ISS to review lifeboat protocols if they have to abandon ship, and no new personnel go into orbit until we know more. Get a group together to monitor telemetry from every satellite we control for effects of its passing on our own planets, especially Mars."

The young woman scribbled rapidly on her tablet and began walking out as she typed.

"And get me the colonel from Space Force who was here last month. His military satellites will be at risk and I don't want him thinking Russia or Korea has attacked." As she slipped into the hallway, the administrator was already calling the head of the Japanese Space Agency himself over an open voice line. They needed to spread the word.

Two days later as the Director sat with his staff, reviewing the latest plots of trajectory, they knew the passing planet would clearly miss the Earth. "It is agreed then, a miss but the cloud of meteors it created will intercept Earth in a little less than two years from today and last for perhaps months on end. Likely we will lose several vital and expensive satellites. I want options on orbital alterations to put them behind the planet when we're hit. What frightens me most is the chance this little planet, no larger than Mercury..." there was a confirming nod from two of the staff, "...might not be alone. If it's a rogue without a star, fine. If not, god help us."

There were more nods around the table.

"Re-direct every observatory telescope we control. Tell ESA and anyone else with eyes. Now that we know its track, look backward at the empty portion of sky this rock came from and see if worse is coming. Do it now."

"Mr. Director," added another staff member just getting off the phone. "US Space Force command has given the object an official name, Xenos. They are efforting what to do if we are wrong about its path missing Earth."

The director of NASA laughed darkly. "If we are wrong and something even half the size of Mercury hits us, we're all dead. Proceed with the best available projections and backtrack this bastard. We must know if there are more right behind it."

***

It wasn't long before New Earth Associates was brought in for consultation. Eric Arvidson and his young cousin Jacquelyn kept watch on data as it poured in from observatories and agencies around the world. The think tank had been coordinating information tasked with assisting satellite launch efforts of private space companies.

They also had a few contracts supporting NASA and ESA. Now perhaps they could put academic plans for intercepting a visitor into action.

Jean Kathryn was on the phone with them almost every day. "Is it close enough or slow enough for us to send a robot to intercept and land there? Is it alone or part of a system? When will we know? Did we get the rights to the Japanese robot-lander that attached itself to that comet three years ago? How fast is it? Can we reach it with our own rocket before it's gone?"

They pumped her for information in return. She was keeping in touch with governments and space agencies at the highest levels. How interested were they? Had politicians dedicated telescope time to studying Xenos? Did anyone else plan an interception launch?

She had quickly convinced the board of her satellite division to send a small, fast robot to intercept the visitor. An expensive mission but possible. They were amazed how many of the systems they pioneered in recent years now fit together so well for a mission of this type. Jean Kathryn was not amazed, but pleased. This was, after all, her father's plan all along. To bide their time. To grow capabilities, then strike when the opportunity arrived.

A few quiet calls to Musk and Branson and several others put real meat on the bones of her plan. Perhaps this would only be a test run, sending a robot to land and travel out of the solar system faster and farther than any Earth ship could bring it: at 40 km/sec! Fabulous. No Earth ships could move that fast for an entire journey between solar systems.

Perhaps this was a chance for more, for people to finally hitch a ride.

It was a few weeks later Earth observatories found a dull brown/red dwarf. A star. And it was on an intercept course with our system just like little Xenos. It was quickly realized Xenos was simply in a distant orbit about the star. And that it was likely there were other closer bodies in orbit, potentially much larger. Within a few months, the star coming to visit would prove to have its own solar system. The press christened it Aurora, after the Roman god of dawn. At New Earth Associates, scientists quickly developed their pet name for it; Janus: god of beginnings, transitions, doorways, and passages. And endings.

***

"This is Grimsby Rogers, hear now the news." His broadcast began like so many before it but quickly grabbed his audience sitting down to dinner or their evening newspapers.

"Astronomers at the Mount Palomar Observatory have announced a star, not our own, is on a path to collide with our solar system. While still a few years away, it is inevitable that its passing will have a profound effect on our own solar system. When asked if this event is related to the appearance of Xenos almost two years ago, scientists were in disagreement..."

People jumped from their chairs. They switched channels. They called friends and family. They tried the internet. All news media and talking heads were broadcasting the same chilling subject.

A star was coming our way.

"Good Evening. This star, smaller than our own, nevertheless has its own group of planets, the exact number still being determined. While there is no present danger, government officials have already scheduled press conferences throughout the week after their own briefings have been completed."

While children were still enjoying lights in the night sky from the Xenos meteors, some parents were now alarmed enough not to allow many outside after sunset, huddling in the imagined safety of their homes. Others could not take their eyes off familiar distant stars in the sky and wondered.

"Umm, oh wow Eric, it has an asteroid belt!" gasped Jacquelyn. "We have to tell Jean Kathryn right away!" The conclusion was unavoidable. Even thru the dust of our Oort cloud and that of the visiting star's cloud of asteroids, initial occultation techniques had finally yielded bare-bones data, the existence of several inner planets (assumed rocky like ours with no gas giants detected).

A solar system was coming and the public now knew it.

She puzzled over the latest cloud density reports from the European space agency. "Is that why we didn't see it until now? Until it was this close? The dust and debris orbiting it?"

Eric concurred, having this morning finished reading the same report. His cousin, only 17, had already shown the intelligence that would mark her life. "Partly, of course. A gas giant would have cleared out a lot of outer dust and meteors like ours did. Also, it's a dim but seemingly steady dwarf star. A lot less light output in the visible spectrum than a star like our Sol so it was easily missed. Still, it has a goldilocks zone warm enough for life, just closer in and therefore with a likely shorter planetary year than our own. Seasons if any will come and go quickly."

Per their training and the long-standing family mission, they send a preliminary report to Jean Kathryn and immediately grabbed all new data they could lay their hands upon with a physical rendezvous in mind. The think tank managers would need hard data to pass on to the planners and engineers building ships. And be practical enough for Jean Kathryn to free up the enormous sums of money any mission would require. It was more than a theoretical exercise now. Actual ship construction, robot operators, and all the rest must begin immediately with current technology. And a lot of money.

***

Jean Kathryn got off the phone after thanking the Chilean observatory manager for giving her a draft of the report he was preparing for a congressional oversight committee.

She immediately called Eric.

"Got something for you, cousin. The Euro ELT observatory is about to issue a report I just emailed you. From what I read in the abstract, they've crunched numbers on five planets. The outermost is Neptune-sized with its 'year' determined to be 70 Earth years or so. Fortunately, it only travels a small arc of its huge orbit anywhere near our solar system. It will miss us by many AU. The star itself and its innermost planets are another matter."

"Eric, you guys have to read the data and tell me."

He already knew what he would be looking for. To answer if any are habitable.

"One of the first things we will ascertain is if the Goldilocks planets are tidally locked," noted Eric. No seasons unless from non-circular planetary orbits. "Strength of its magnetic field of course. And how much rotational tilt, if any? Most of our planets tilt to some degree except for Uranus oddly spinning on its side! Remember? If they have one side only facing their sun from tidal locking, a planet like that could present more than just landing difficulties. Life as we know it likes steady seasons."
Jacquelyn sat nearby listening. She knew our moon was locked to the Earth that way, always showing us the same face, causing her to interject hopefully, "...difficulties but possibilities for energy production at the light/dark equator we never had on Earth. And maybe year-round cultivation on the light side, perhaps using sub-surface greenhouses to give the soil rest for periodic fertilization after a harvest." Eric knew this was a specific interest of the young engineering savant from her master's thesis at Columbia University.

The idea that on the tidal-locked moon, you could generate power without burning fossil or other fuels simply by pumping fluid back and forth across the light/dark boundary, or using Sterling engines, was as old as science fiction itself.

She also had in mind an old engineering paper done in a 1970s master's thesis for a vertical 'tornado turbine' which looked like a hollow cylindrical skyscraper whose windows were louvers: solid plates hinged to swing in and create a tornado-shaped vortex inside the empty cylinder, with a turbine safely anchored at ground-level underneath the point of the funnel. No fuel. No pumping. An interesting idea, but winds on Earth were not high enough for viability. Given a tidally locked side always facing a star, and a bitter night side always in darkness, one could expect low altitude winds at extreme velocities crossing from the night to light sides. Our moon had no atmosphere so no winds, but these new worlds…she wondered.

With enough power, anything could be achieved, ultimately.

"We need updates on the atmospheric numbers as they come in. We're gathering data wherever published, but governments are already starting to delay some observatory findings to give themselves an edge. An edge for what I don't know!"

"What do you need most, cousin?"

"Anything you can get us on radiation levels experienced at the surface of those planets. Atmospheric spectroscopy too – carbon, water vapor, oxygen, methane levels. The works. Are you certain there are four candidate planets, no moons?"

"Yes, the report said only four, but no one has ruled out tiny moons as Mars possesses. Still too far away to find them by occultation techniques against their star or planetary perturbation."

"And it's too far to tell if any or all of the four planets have an electromagnetic field like Earth, I get it, so maybe liquid iron cores and maybe not. There's still a lot we won't know until it's too late to act upon. Jean Kathryn, we have to make assumptions and live with them."

She sat upright. "Then we don't wait. We assume viability and prepare several ships. For now, just one intercept ship to drop a lander on the best candidate for data before it passes. And one straight panspermia ship of bacteria, spores, tardigrades, plants, fish, and lower insects. It will cost a small fortune, but I can sell it."

Her voice went to gravel as she uttered that which her own board had never heard her say.

"If we detect a breathable atmosphere somewhere, then all bets are off. We launch a crash program – if you'll pardon the expression – to send as many transit colony ships with people as we can manage. Human volunteers to take off on an intercept course. The ships will also contain a wide sampling from the Svalbard Global Seed Vault, mostly food, textile, and drug-related crops." These Arvidson planners knew there would be no turning back when colonists got there even if it was found untenable like Venus or Mars.

Eric injected a disheartening note. "We'll know well before launching people if it turns out the atmospheres are poisonous or some other consideration renders them inhabitable. But you'll have blown a lot of the family's fortune on rockets that never launch. Company directors will lynch you, and stockholders will provide the rope when all their dividends are cut to zero!"

"I know. But you know we can't wait until we're sure. I'll start on the robot intercept ship now, so that will launch no matter what. But we won't launch a transit colony ship until we know more. Get me your best plans to date. I'll start building them tomorrow, but I promise no one will be sent to certain death."

After they hung up, Jacqueline interjected, "And Eric, please let us remember to confirm the panspermia inventory also includes mangrove and octopus. I know they were not part of the initial plan but if there are swamps or saltwater oceans..."

Pausing a moment, she asked him, "...think anyone will go?"

***

Jean Kathryn had spent her energies of the past ten years securing control of her father's vast legacy. Now 28 and a mother of two herself, she ran the primary holding company with trusted presidents in each of the industrial lines she controlled. Petrochemicals, aviation, transport, and even several medical supply companies and research labs. The family fortune was secure. Now, holding Eric's report in her hands about this visitor to our solar system, her mind shifted to her father's conversation years ago and the legacy it represented. She would not fail him.

There was an unhappy board of directors seated on the top floor of the Arvidson Holding Company building. Oaken panels darkened the walls to the demeanor of those now seated at the table. The table itself was darker still, of heavy black walnut selected by the founder himself.

"You're going to do what?!" Her attorneys and board, loyal men and women who were key to wresting control into her own hands in more than name only, were shocked by her announcement. "On this preliminary evidence?"

"I have more data thanks to New Earth Associates and our government contracts. We're putting an all-out effort into studying this interstellar object, including another satellite rendezvous mission to intercept and tag it before it gets here. We're the only ones who can. NASA and the ESA started committing their limited funds and staff only 2 years ago to a new lunar mission and landing men on Mars. No way they can pivot and reassign the kind of ship needed for this in time before it passes. It's us or no one."

"The expense will be frightening.....to actually land biologic material on another world and hope it will survive!"

Laughing to herself but stone-faced, 'If they think this expensive, they'll really hate the next part. That of sending ships loaded with human life to seed a world. The idea of people jumping to a passing planet or moon-sized body? They would think she'd gone crazy. She better wait until more data came in for that final step.

Was she crazy? Was it too soon in our technological adolescence to make the attempt? Eric's studies at the think tank said no, they could do it with current tech. But the distances had to be just-so, the size of the planet so-and-so, and a dozen other critical requirements just to have a chance at tagging it, no less sending anyone.

Blow a third of the family wealth on such a venture by selling off entire divisions, yes indeed, insane. She knew she was crazy enough to do it. Would anyone else be crazy enough to go? To board colony ships if a body appeared in reach with just the right atmosphere, temperature, water content, etc. That was, after all the ultimate vision of Bobby Arvidson. A lifeboat for humans safely away from Earth.

***

Nearly two years later, Earth was being peppered with a meteor storm without equal. If this was the result of a single small planet, their 'Pluto', passing close by, what would happen when the rest arrived in another three years? Just three short years to prepare. One of her companies had succeeded in launching a robot probe to Xenos, landing there and transmitting data as it sped away. But the public and governments panicking themselves were focused in the other direction.

They looked towards oncoming Aurora and its inner planetary family.

"Good evening. As reported earlier, we can now confirm the meteor shower caused by the rogue planet Xenos is actually the leading edge of this distant threat." People tuned into their most trusted sources, either on the web or the pulpit. Newscasters gave them facts but were mostly limited to repeating what was already known of Xenos. The pulpit gave them assurances of divine plans, but punishment for the wicked.

Turning off the television, and stretching out of bed to summon her personal assistant, the head of the Arvidson empire donned fuzzy bear-feet slippers and begged for a glass of pineapple-orange juice.

"More bad news on the news, ma'am?"

She nodded without answering as the cold juice woke up her senses. The glass was so delightfully cold condensation tickled her palm.

"Should make it easier to get recruits for your colony."

Not immediately agreeing, Jean Kathryn was introspective. "I was thinking of those who died fleeing Europe after the Americas were discovered. There always seemed to be far safer options for anyone with the intelligence, health, and skill-sets demanded of such a colony. My own concerns are that the 'experts' we have been relying upon have come up with better than academic studies. These are working plans now and lives are at stake."

"Perhaps," mused her aged companion, one who seemed to anticipate the need for juice or a moment of silence without fail, "...perhaps more than just the lives on the ship are at stake, eh ma'am?"

Jean Kathryn's eyes narrowed at hearing the truth again from this trusted retainer. An agreeing nod and the sleepy mother was on her way to becoming what she had to be, now and always. For everyone concerned.

Robert Arvidson's idea had always been to have them design a mission or missions using present technology only, then continuously improve designs without building anything and modify over the years as advances were made in engines, robotics, germination, and hibernation techniques, and the lot. Less than 20 years since his original concept, they would have to go with whatever tech was currently available. So soon!

And so many ifs. This first intercept scout mission had succeeded and cost a small fortune all by itself, caught up to and landed safely on Xenos. It gave them vital data encouraging the idea of a colony effort. Now, with spectroscope data from observatories and satellites the world over, vital atmospheric data was coming in on the inner planets.

This actually could happen in her lifetime.

"Colonists? The way things are now on Earth? The last few years of coastal flooding have sunk a piece of several major cities and fires wiped out numerous villages and towns all over the world. Radiation levels from a depleted ozone layer are rising. We may have done enough to turn around climate change and stabilize the polar ice caps, but maybe not. Any number of small regional wars erupting over resources like oil and metals could turn into something completely out of control. And that was before this surprise arrival. People are freaked. Yeah, a whole lot of qualified people will take the shot. Just in case."

She hoped.

An assistant waiting downstairs heard her hope. He had been staffed just to screen candidates. As they walked together to the car, he stated, "Let us not forget minor damage from all the small meteors we've been getting sprinkled with after that first planet creamed thru our asteroid belt. Xenos is thru and gone but a third of the displaced material coming here was big enough and rocky enough to make it to the surface. Not burn up. And that was just the leading edge of their planetary system. That's an incentive."

"It's coming close. Even if nothing big in our system gets hit directly by something big of theirs, the gravity distortions could wreak havoc for decades to come. Longer."

"Yes, Eric and his gang will be recalculating asteroid and cometary orbits for a generation. Maybe more." Contingent on if we were even still here. She refocused on their mission. "Ships with ion engines will have to have enough juice to slightly alter course to intercept any of the candidate planets once on final approach. Chemical burst engines on standby. We won't know the exact destination at launch! Ion drives aren't enough alone, impulse too low. Haven't heard anything concerning moons. If they have something like a Europa or Enceladus or Titan it might prove a better candidate than the inner goldilocks planets. Once we launch, we're committed. Changes to an intercept course will be limited."

"Sure, but the preliminary orbital estimates I've seen say their moons will be too small to be viable, smaller than Titan. Wouldn't they have seen larger ones by now? That will be confirmed one way or the other before summer. Good news for Earth, but bad news if we like the looks of any of its moons."

They realized it would have to be their inner worlds, then. Four chances.

They pulled into the New Earth Associates parking garage and made their way to the central conference room. Eric tried to be realistic about their prospects for his cousin by saying, "And there's no possibility that we can resupply them. They find they need just one more tech or something not on board, or more of it until they were established, they're out of luck. Our best cargo ship – even no more people, just robots – can't be fast enough to catch them. Our transit ships have to be out front as the planets catch up to them. No re-supply even if we're still in business here."

Later he sat with Jacqueline as they both stepped back from daily reports and engineering tasks to just think a while. To see if there was some big picture item they'd missed.

Something which would doom the colony before it started.

"Jean Kathryn broke out the folders today. Invoked the liquidation protocols. She'll contact all the groups whose support we'll need to get this off the ground in time. And concerning political relations, the time will come soon to call in every favor we have. And remember founder Bobby's admonition that each third-party group should be kept blissfully unaware that we're working directly with those other groups as long as we can, or at least minimize them. They each have to feel 'ownership'. That they are special."

They both thought a moment quietly.

Jacqueline happily intoned, "I'm glad we get to leave the politics to her."

***

The director of the American SETI program was belaboring the loss of prestige and funding. After the collapse of the Arecibo Radio Telescope, funding and interest were harder every year. Only a small bump occurred two years ago when news came in of the small, dangerous planet from outside our solar system. He was sitting quietly wondering about another almost useless fundraising trip to Washington when several of his staff burst into his office.

"It's coming. Not just the little planet causing all these meteor showers, but a star. An entire star passing close by."

He and they immediately saw a chance to finally communicate with another world, even if for only a brief period.

"All this time. Listening for signals at least 10 or 50 or 100 years old for some signs of life. Now something right in our neighborhood! Even one light year away means real communication. A weak signal never meant for us, like television or radio programs, could be heard clearly. And answered!"

"If someone is there, they may have already heard our television or radio broadcasts…"

"…and answered! Yes! Redirect radio-telescope searches from broad random patterns to focus on the path of the visiting star. Get updated software for all our translation programs, language adapters, and Fourier-Gaussian analysis of signals for pattern recognition."

"If they are not yet aware of us," he said standing, "their signals will be weak and omni-directional like ours. Record everything, even patterns from the star itself to be filtered out as noise later. And get me our biggest donors list! Move like you have a purpose, people!"

***

A related group, Messaging Extraterrestrial Intelligence (METI) International, was laughed at in 2018 when they sent an encoded message into space labeled "Sonar Calling GJ273b," which the organization aimed at a red dwarf known as Luyten's Star, 12 lightyears from Earth. They too now received funding from a quiet think tank that expressed solidarity with their goals.

"This arrival within our solar system would cut transmission distances from light-years to orbital years! We might do more than hear if they are broadcasting video or radio. We could send and perhaps get a response before they moved on. And vice versa!"

Debate raged over what to send or say. For the past half dozen decades, Earth technology had us glowing unintentionally in the radio and other regions of the electromagnetic spectrum like a small sun. For METI this was their time to shine. And with the new money from that anonymous project in California, they could focus their signal broadcast efforts on a very small part of the sky indeed.

They also received very public death threats. Obvious fears erupted in the media as some survivalist groups who never looked at the sky above their mountain cabin or desert hideaway retreats now screamed at METI to stop their broadcasts! What if passing aliens heard us and came here to take our Earth? What if this was not a chance visit but a planned invasion? There were scuffles and harassment. Fear spread in every imaginable way including religious revivals and new prophets. For some, it was proof of their prophecies of Armageddon and biblical revelations. This became the form the end would take and only the righteous would survive or be saved.

And, of course, there were the evangelists who saw this as an opportunity to spread the word. Among the most strident and politically active religious groups, a few were contacted by New Earth Associates. They were encouraged to pressure public officials to assemble crash programs to reach the new worlds with dedicated believers on board, citing how traditional European explorers always had clerics aboard to convert the heathen. When New Earth Associates revealed to them how far their plans had progressed, massive support both political and economic was forthcoming in return for Arvidson assurances of their sect participation and influence. Empty assurances.

**

"You know as well as I do that the idea to send bacteria or

primitive life to seed other solar systems is a pipe dream in this century. We don't have the engines, the funds, and if you spent the money with what we have, it would be decades before anything reaches another world. We'd likely never know what became of them. Who's going to shell out money for that?"

All the astrophysicists at the conference knew intimately the distances to the nearest star systems. Alpha Centauri at 4 lightyears, Barnard's star at 12, and all the others in our 50-lightyear neighborhood.

"Now we don't need interstellar ships! A set of planets are coming to us! If we build fast enough, if we get plans off blackboards and find someone or some government to actually build the ships, can we get to a passing planet in time? Before it leaves the solar system?"

"If it leaves without wrecking us as it passes."

"What could this intruder do even if it missed Earth? What would our sun's gravity do to the orbit of its worlds?" Of all people, they knew well how fragile a balance orbital mechanics were. How our apparently stable solar system of planets, moons, and comets sat on a knife-edge of gravitational balances established over billions of years. They all had opinions.

"No way I'd try to get to another planet like this."

"All the more reason to build a lifeboat. Even something just to orbit the Earth until the danger has passed. Right now, we have nothing. Worse than nothing – a pair of 10-man space stations that need constant parts and re-supply from Earth. We need an alternative!"

"I'm ready to go. To try for a new world. I'm frightened by what I'm seeing so far. The media is loaded with responses by the public, and by government officials, of invasions, and divine punishments, and the whole thing is considered fake news by our political enemies. Damned little responsible discussion on who has a good space program. Who can build a lifeboat in time? Who can manufacture ships to escape Earth if it's hit? We have to find out. We have to get in touch with some real programs and make government officials see there are real solutions."

As always, they feared human mobs more than natural catastrophes. But this catastrophe could easily eclipse primitive human attempts to destroy ourselves. Most men and women at this conference believed in no actions by gods, just nature. Yet this natural danger was real, if not certain, and must be dealt with. These individuals cast about for someone doing more than praying or shaking their fists. A number of them found and turned to the panspermia projects. And an odd little think tank.

***

Military establishments worldwide had little to say publicly. The men at this table had spent a lifetime ensuring what was discussed here went to no other ears.

"Frankly, for me, the danger is nothing we can do anything about if the rogue star hits us directly, or directly enough. The same pertains to a collision with any of the planets orbiting it."

"Then what's our role?"

There were smiles around the table.

"The current shower of small meteors. Spot on for our goals. Yes, we've always lobbied for increased space force budgets. Now, we must be ready in three years with interceptors against dangerous meteors dislodged in this alien flyby. Only a little lead time remains. Those showers from that first planet, the Hawaiian named one, were bad enough. All the scientists agree the rest of this solar system passing will be far worse."

"Heaven sent." There were nods of agreement.

Privately, many military minds did not believe anything more than the dust and a sprinkling of car-size rocks would ever come to pass, still in denial against an enemy they could not see or mentally wrap their heads around. Just a few rocks in pretty nighttime displays for the civilians. A few fires in a few cities. Maybe a tidal wave or two.

Yet these leaders saw a practical side: an excuse to deploy and arm space platforms, long designed to intimidate other nations on Earth but never politically expedient to get approved. Now was their chance to gain an edge for themselves under the guise of world unity and planetary defense.

***

The think tank founder's daughter, laughed as she sat on the floor of her father's library with young children of her own. "Why are you laughing Mommy?"

Jean Kathryn laughed at the wisdom of Robert Arvidson and held his mantle of authority firmly in both youthful hands. Not for her children or her children's future children, but for her. This danger and this chance surprisingly came in her time and she would bend the will of all around her to achieve those ends. She knew in her heart what all the power structures would be up to; scientists, political-religious leaders, the military. She kept stacking the deck in her favor the best she could.

Perhaps it would work and mankind would spread into a new solar system. Perhaps it would fail and brave would-be colonists would die en masse. Plenty died to cross the Atlantic in wind-powered sailing vessels. Entire colonies arrived but died of disease, starvation, or Indian attack. And that was at a time when a whole lot of people still thought they would fall off the end of the Earth! Perhaps only colonists would survive as the Earth was destroyed or rendered inhabitable.

Or the best possibility: both a colony and old Earth would continue with mankind having a foothold in both.

If it went the other way, if Earth were doomed and any

colonization mission failed to find a home elsewhere, well, she would not entertain those thoughts. What would it matter if that were true? Her children wrestled with her and climbed playfully one over the other like she was a living mountain, each wanting to be king of the hill.

She would act for them.

Arvidsons had always acted. She would try, and keep trying at all costs even if it bankrupted the family here. If the Earth survived, the family could always start over from near nothing if need be, and succeed. This was her belief. They had in the past and would again.

Either way, she smiled remembering how it began. "You were right, father. I can see them all. All the power groups. I can almost hear them! What they want. How far they will go in fear or greed. Just like you must have in your day." And she laughed again in front of her puzzled but smiling children.

***

The first launches to put ships into near-Earth orbits came and went without too much fanfare. Most were public launches from various governments aimed at taking scientific measurements and sending communication probes to be in a position to orbit the passing bodies. It seemed some agency or private company made a launch every week. Several bearing the Arvidson logo were quietly more ambitious, launching unspecified cargo and robots on a long intercept course.

Military establishments made test launches of new kinetic energy and mass driver weapons to divert or destroy imagined threats. And a new generation of panspermia ships was being built by governments to send spores and seeds off-planet, but most would not be completed in time to rendezvous with this pass by. Perhaps the next? Or a mission to Mars or Saturn's moon Titan?

It is an exciting time for every governmental and private space agency on the planet, and the public was torn between fear and reassurance, glued to their cable channels. The star would miss us, that was certain. But what of its effects? Social media was frequently overloading network capacity. It reminds those old enough of the first human landing on the moon. But darkly riveting. This televised show could reach out and bite us.

"Good Evening. At the press conference today, officials discounted every question about building an orbital lifeboat or ship to carry people to one of the new worlds as it passes. Nothing official has come out of foreign space agencies either. However, sources within several agencies acknowledge plans have been underway under tight wraps to do just that. To wait it out onboard a temporary lifeboat, or to actually hitch a ride to another part of the galaxy."

By and large, the public stuck to their governmental announcements of safety and their local religious upbringing that the Creator of the universe knows what he's doing and will protect us, we who are made in his image. For a planet where 80% or more of the adult humans believe in some sort of afterlife and a god or gods, how much more was it to ask that this too was all part of a divine plan? That it would all work out. Even non-believers held place since it seemed far too little time left to do more.

With every press conference, every month that Aurora and her planets came closer, congregations of all denominations swelled, as did their coffers.

***

Only six months before the first transit ship launch was to occur, things were not as blindly optimistic at the Arvidson think tank. Eric paced and almost shouted into his headset, gesturing with one hand while waving a sheath of printouts at the unseeing phone with the other.

"No, no, no! We have to know now! By the time the new Chinese telescope reports atmospheric density and temperature variations on the four inner worlds this fall, it will be too late." Pausing for moments, Jacquelyn read in Eric's face the ineffective response without hearing it.

"You're not hearing me," continued Eric, "The two best planets are tidally locked, like our Moon. We are going to land at a twilight equator; that's decided. Listen, if the substellar side nearest the sun is not cooled by enough of an atmosphere, we can create power from the 300km winds as hot air rises and goes north into the dark half, while cold air screams to the substellar side at ground level using Savonius windmills; no sweat. But if the atmosphere is thick enough to moderate the temperature difference between the halves, we're better off pumping fluids between the day to night sides through the twilight zone and having power that way. Or, if there is no atmosphere for enough surface winds and the two sides have a 500-700 degree differential, the ASRG Sterling thermionic generators can make power with no moving parts or pumping. We land at the edge of darkness and light."

"But we can't transport all three systems!" Taking a breath as Jacquelyn gently fluttered her hands to have him slow down, he completed the call with, "We have to choose one system and chose it now! This week. Much more time passes and we'll never intercept the planets. We need this data. Just make the decision!"

As he hung up his cousin tapped his shoulder and to his surprise offered a handful of Mallomars. His tension melted in a chuckle as they both devoured the taste of marshmallow and chocolate treats, musing on how far they'd come in the five years since Xenos appeared.

Jacquelyn offered, "You know the crew teams are planning to take at least one small unit of each 3 systems. Once the primary choice is loaded, whatever spare room they have will be crammed with parts for the other two!"

She smiled and Eric smiled back. "I know. But the Webb telescope team doesn't need to know. I wanted to push them. Hard." He took a long breath and nodded. "They'll come up with the highest probability in time for launch."

Growing serious again, Jacquelyn noted, "We still don't know which planet to target, and likely won't by launch time. Spectrophotometers showed one with definite chlorophyll signatures in an O2 atmosphere, and the other had traces of wood combustion products." She shrugged. "Forest fires or pre-industrialization? We may have to leave the final choice of planet to the crew on approach. And their instruments."

***

The men and women selected from a surprisingly large pool of qualified candidates now lived at the construction facilities. They oversaw all stages of transit ship construction. They oversaw the engineers and biologists making out the cargo inventory. Whatever you take with you is all you are going to have.

George Arvidson sat with his command crew at one end of the long conference table, with Warren Arvidson and his team at the other. "After dropping the chemical boosters, the pair of transit ships have two stages to work with: a nuclear ion first stage to get where we want efficiently using the new 1300sec specific impulse engines, and chemical retro engines in the nose of the second stage to slow and orbit our craft."

Warren chimed in pointing to the schematic blown up on the wall. "Between the two engines the elongated body of the cargo: a simple shell containing 5 separate landing vehicles. Upon orbital approach, the ion engines will be shut down and chemical rockets in the nose ignited, slowing each transit ship for the calculated orbital slot. Making use of an idea gotten from the Russian concept of switching the nuclear output from engine to vehicle support upon arrival, on achieving orbit the nuclear first stage would be left in a geosynchronous orbit over the target planet above the landing site at the twilight equator."

George's First Mate rose and continued the update. "Using the glider method of American space shuttles, the 5 landing vehicles will separate from the chemical retro engine and begin individual oneway trips to the surface. Each contains both people and supplies and can be re-linked on the ground by deploying flexible tunnels once on the surface. This will be the initial outpost, one from each transit ship. The two outposts would be set up as close to each other as our pilots can achieve. In all, the two transit ships contained 10 landing modules and are sized for 73 x 2 pairs of young adult humans, plus one child per pair."

None of the children were their own for improved genetic diversity.

A week came when a pair of government-built ships took off from two different continents with high international publicity. Their original missions for which they had been built had been scrubbed. One was now called a panspermia seed ship with no humans aboard but robotic controllers to make their attempt. Just spores and seeds and bacteria and plankton. The other was a slightly more chancy operation involving something more, living complex organisms, from land-based plants and tardigrades up to small ocean life. The ocean life included types for freshwater, saltwater, octopuses with copper-based blood instead of iron, and even the odd sulfur eaters of the deep volcanic environs on Earth. They were met with a combination of public cheering and worry. At least life on Earth had a chance of springing up elsewhere as it had here. Thus we might not completely come to an end if things went bad.

"I'm proud of this part. My people in Ukraine came up with the original concept." The two First Mates were comparing notes as they toured the fifth module assembly area.

"All landing vehicles in each ship had an identical cargo of people and supplies, except this last in the set. This fifth lander contains a microwave receiving pad, whose mesh would be radar targeted by the nuclear stage still in orbit and collect energy beamed down as microwaves." His counterpart smiled in agreement. "Brilliant. In this manner, colonists will have an immediate and substantial source of electric power in those critical first months while erecting our homestead before ground-based power units are deployed and operable. It could mean the difference."

A surprise for the public came six months later when news media reported that several more ships had just launched. Two much larger transit ships using ion engines, built quietly in orbit over the past few years, were all but complete. The current launches of simple chemical rockets into orbit were its supplies and equipment. And crew. And as the last stage is attached externally to sections built in orbit, it would boost a large transit ship out of Earth's orbit before falling away.

The transit ships were finally fully manned. New Earth Associates had originally thought to copy the enormous Russian MK-700 multistage rockets which were designed to be assembled in orbit. This technology was well understood and upgraded when NASA came out several years later with its own Copernicus MTV (Mars Transfer Vehicle) design, also intended to be constructed in orbit. These now loaded with crew and cargo were improved by efforts of the think tank, using the latest in composite materials and multistage bimodal engine operation.

Already aboard, Mary Ryan sat with two young Arvidson children and the rest under ten in the kindergarten area. A combination of little red schoolhouse, infirmary, and library, the children would be sequestered here and repeatedly briefed on what was expected of them. Mary loved children, having birthed four of her own on Earth, and now found herself the eldest of several nurses and matrons watching over this next generation. Most were still strapped into their seats where they could watch displays of the bridge crew in action and video scans of the Earth below. There were even video links from the pair of all-robotic panspermia vessels which preceded them into space.

The two young Arvidsons sitting on Mary's lap, however, need more consolation for a tearful parting from a much loved mother on Earth than they needed more data.

"This is your legacy, children. You are Arvidsons. Your blood built this. Your mother, Jean Kathryn, your grandfather who started it all, and all the aunts, uncles, and cousins who put everything they had into making this possible. When your time comes, you too will have the bravery to succeed. Maybe the Earth itself will continue after things settle down. We'll be in touch by radio waves...how fast are they?"

Both together smiled ironically, "Speed of light, 3 times 105th km/sec". Come on, Nana Mary, we knew that when we were 9!" All measurements on board were in metric units to forestall confusion, irrespective of the country or culture of origin of the crew. It was part of the daily drills to become fluent in math and critical scientific constants.

The young boy, a male image of his mother, asked in genuine interest, "If Earth doesn't make it." He glanced quickly at his sister. "If everyone there dies, will you be the oldest human alive, Nana?"

Mary hesitated only a moment without change of expression. She had long been used to and delighted in things children would ask. When her own grandson, now grown to be a scientist, was small and would ask questions about astronomy far beyond his or Mary's ken, she would answer him as fully and accurately as she could, in adult language, and not dumb it down for a child. So she continued to do so here. Her long-dead husband used to chide her on that account, for why explain things which he couldn't possibly understand at his age? She always gave the same answer. One day he will. And he will grow up without fairy tales. As long as she gave it straight, even though she did not know an answer, he always skipped away satisfied and happy.

"You may be right, Robert. But let's not rush things. Earth may manage to survive the expected bombardment and gravity swings as the new sun passes by. Come closer." They both snuggled with her, and she knew their thoughts were still with their mother on Earth.

"You will both make her so proud to use the chance she has given us all."

***

"We interrupt our usual program to announce that people have been launched into orbit on four enormous chemical rockets. They appear to be heading to a rendezvous with two other ships. Two ships built right in orbit!"
He turned down the television. "Oh, well. It had to come out sometime. We spent a lot on the best security money could buy."

Jacqueline was unconcerned. "Cheer up, Eric. They launched. They're gone. The crew sizes were enormous compared to previous launches and had to be noticed."

They listened along with a nervous public to further news reports live from various launch pads that each ship had more than 40 pairs of humans, young adults in age. Not just pilots and a few scientists. Each also contained an unknown number of preschool children, perhaps as many as one per pair of adults. One reporter uncovered the uncomfortable fact that many geneticists felt 73 was the required number to avoid inbreeding damage in people. The lessons of the Vikings in Greenland

and other cultures throughout history were quoted. This news caught public attention and spread like wildfire.

This is when the trouble really began.

Many people felt they were being abandoned. Governmental trust was at a century-long low anyway before the arrival, and once their desperate desire to believe governmental assurances of safety was cracked, it quickly shattered into street riots. The most damaging rumor was that government top brass was likely saving itself or its own offspring. And impossible to disprove!

Violence escalated. Many people in cities simply stayed home and left their jobs. Some say they want to avoid the violence. Others just wonder why they should bother if it really was all ending.

But the two transit ships could be gone before protests or government actions interfered. As soon as final supplies had arrived aboard, the two Captains broke Earth orbit for a moon orbit at their own discretion. Given that position, a moon orbit would sling them after the already fast-moving panspermia and cargo vessels. A little more time in orbit for last-minute preparation was desirable but the Arvidson captains were in agreement and thus they radioed Jean Kathryn: that it was safer to go with what they had right away.

"We must get to the rendezvous point before the planets do. Leaving now buys us a small cushion."

Jean Kathryn listened to them while watching her monitors. She was seeing a teleconference of Congressional hearings, insisting the government alone was authorized to decide who could go and when. The public will be informed in due time. She watched on a second television the U.N. proceedings where joint international efforts were being proposed for lifeboats to orbit the Earth and were being quickly rejected as ridiculously expensive. Tempers flared.

Mission Commanders George and Warren Arvidson aboard their ships hung on the line. There was only a two-second voice delay at this distance, but the seconds dragged into minutes. Thinking of the children she would never see again, Jean Kathryn commanded;

"Leave now. Your discretion for launch at best possible speed."

Arvidson agents viewed the transit ship exhausts from the ISS, rapidly growing smaller as they headed to swing around the moon. There were quite a few Arvidsons aboard each colony vessel, but many stayed at their terrestrial jobs and after this hurried launch turned their attention 180 degrees about to renew their Earth-bound projects.

If the Earth were not destroyed, if life here continued, they wished to pick up the pieces and not see a fall into total barbarism after present social upheavals ran their course. If Earth were destroyed, well, they had implemented a possible solution and done all in their power to give humans a chance elsewhere. SETI had detected no alien broadcasts, but there was always doubt in the public mind. Space stations would continue to monitor transmissions from the transit colony ships and relay those reports to a panicked Earth.

Governments were now powerless to stop the broadcasts as doing so would infuriate an already alarmed public. To stay in power, they had to appear in charge, and lend at least verbal support to the surprise missions.

Bobby Arvidson's only child had placed both her own son and daughter aboard one transit ship. Both ships contained many cousins. Feeling relief at the completion of the great task, Jean Kathryn looked up as they left Earth orbit, smiled in her fuzzy slippers, and blew them a kiss from the floor of her father's aged library.

###

VEIL OF DREAMS

The Ethereals

West had often wondered if the majority of humans ever paused to consider how insignificant their dreams were in relation to their waking life. If particularly intense, people again and again seldom spent the rest of a day mulling over the meaning of a particularly unusual dream. Ultimately they seem to dismiss them all as the simple memory processing technique that modern science has currently labeled them. Assured them. Nothing of which to be frightened. Children, stronger right-brained than most adults, take most remembered dreams to heart and run to a parent for solace or understanding, only to be told 'it was just a dream'. Early humans without the benefits of modern science felt much the same.

Just a dream wasn't how West felt. He knew the run-of-the-mill natural memory processing or stress response dreams which were the most common. Even dogs had them, humorously observed running after a rabbit that got away in their waking life. But now and then he experienced another kind. One more intense, yet diffused from relation to our world. West was the last person one might expect to believe there was something to such dreams, as he himself was neither religious, superstitious, nor followed what he considered the ridiculous crutches that most humans embraced, from astrology to gods to lucky rabbit's feet. Yet he thought afterward about the meaning of these odd rarities, also thinking that assigning meaning to dreams was just what those kinds of people would do. The ones that believed in lucky numbers, or an afterlife. It embarrassed him to think he was one of those, being a scientist most of his life but was forced by reason and logic to confront the possibility that the beliefs and superstitions of other humans felt the same to them as his certainty that the ethereal world he occasionally perceived at the edge of consciousness was more than it appeared.

He occasionally wondered if others dreamt as he did, saw the visions he saw in deep sleep, but knew from bitter experience it was likely a futile desire. As a child, he had such dreams more often and being a trusting boy, first related them to his roommate older brother. Being frightened by what he heard, his brother had of course done what older brothers do and betrayed him to his parents. His mom came to him more than once, when his brother heard something particularly disturbing and asked what he dreamt. To her gentle prodding, he tried in vain to relate what he saw and felt but lacked the words. Even in adulthood, it was too difficult to put into a language based on the 'real' world. The closest he heard was in the poetry of Pink Floyd's 'Comfortably Numb', and thought that poet must have experienced this himself as a child. Even artists who worked in the abstract, in cubism, in exotic surrealism, usually failed to correctly express the joy and wonder of that other world, the power which seemed to flow from every poorly defined object perceived in it, and how he felt when immersed inside that universe of power and knowledge. Perhaps Lovecraft could have expressed it well.

His mother and brother both exchanged puzzled glances and failed to grasp even the most rudimentary aspects of what the 6 year old tried to relate. It was better, he realized, to deny the dreams and embrace what passed for normal life. It was already difficult enough being one of them, as his father had long since given up on trying to relate to this his youngest son, a boy physically weaker but far more intelligent than the rest of them, a mystery from where he had popped up in their gene pool. The blue-collar father stood back from the few early encounters like these, leaving them to his compassionate wife, and prayed for the intellectual boy to 'outgrow' whatever this was.

Over the course of his life, West thought himself lucky enough to have been born into the technological society of the 20th century. In due course, he saw men land on the moon and possessed over 100 computers; desktops, laptops, servers, and various small pads. Possessed is the word because owned has a connotation of legal purchase or gift, and most of these were not. Since 2003, one can safely say his entire asset base consisted of stolen items. Then came cyber theft: why not information as well? Cyber information was currency in his day and age.

Early on, and knowing knowledge was power and another form of money, he sought out such knowledge. Knowing also that computers were his friends and followed him around like puppies. Looking online, he came across a few interesting websites and documents with data, but needed bags of it. That's when he hit on the idea to go to work for the IRS. Records galore. Name, address, SSN, dob, the works. And having no felonies on him, he slipped in past their employee security screening at the Department of State easily, working for them inside the firewalls for over a year. Later he found another data rich gold mine in County Clerk websites throughout the US. Free online documents, mostly in pdf or tiff format, gave him everything he needed to apply for credit cards, store cards, bank accounts, and even loans. When tax returns were noted in the news as being vulnerable to identity thieves, West looked into it; soon this became his most profitable gambit.

As a solitary one-man operator, his risks of betrayal by associates and arrest were minimized. Sure, he had a stripper in Raleigh collecting documents for him online and paid her well. And a young single mother in Long Island, another in Elizabeth City, then later in Georgia provided him similar services, plus the usual customary benefits of having such sexually active but vulnerable young women in close and intimate proximity. Everyone benefited and they were universally disappointed when he left a state after 2 or 3 years having exhausted the local assets of UPS mailboxes and local banks with less than adequate security. He was Uncle West or some other nom-de-jure to them and their kids (if any), a family title which he wore with pride. He was a good 'uncle', encouraging and gentle outside the bedroom as was his mother before him. In his retirement, he kept the 'West' name.

After a life without a single felony conviction, in his semi-retirement, the plan was to find an electronic Silk Road at which to dispose by sale his accumulated identities. He would no longer need to use them. As of the decision to retire, he had 1,848 social security numbers, and 350 of them matched with drivers' license numbers. Including a date of birth making each set what he calls a 'triple', of which there were 175. These should have a decent value in cash. Payments would be made onto a debit card or by BitCoin, whichever seems more secure at the time. Thus he never met his buyers.

Now in his 60s, he realized internet and general computer security were beginning to pass him by. His window was spent, and that was ok. Deciding to get out before he slipped up or some new technology tripped him, he spent many a pleasant hour sipping single malt scotch poolside, playing solitary golf and bocce, and studying the latest scientific advances. He kept his hands active in throwing knives or axes and picking a basket full of padlocks. Oddly enough, West was a legitimate scientific consultant who after two marriages decided there was more to life than living in a cubicle and making other men or governments bags of money. But he retained his lifelong love of science and math and kept up with advances in astronomy, the physics of energy production – which was his specialty – and SETI activities in the effort to find intelligent signals. Yes, that could be how he would spend his waning years. Enjoy books, old movies, music, and a host of solitary but non-criminal activities.

He knew all too well the dangers of human pair bonding. His last roommate, a six-foot-tall 19-year-old black coed, was a sexual playground for seven months and a demanding pain in the ass for two more. If nothing else, she confirmed that he would be happier without such relationships, just company when he wanted, none when he didn't, and certainly none with his last name.

West was saddened but oddly calm as he wrote a final email to a best friend from childhood. After 30 years apart, they met again thru the internet, then met in person to share a coffee and catch up. It was clear his friend had surrendered to his catholic Italian wife, had surrendered to an unhappy construction business barely afloat, had surrendered to the shame of making one weak and ADD seeming son, one sacrilegious gay son, and one bisexual daughter who surprisingly went her particular way in this world (good for her, thought West). This onetime dear friend was now trying to 'save' West by introducing him to some manipulator of weak minds who made a business of creating more born again idiots. West declined and left their only meeting never to see his childhood friend again.

West was enjoying lounging about the pool in the company of a young couple he had befriended moving some heavy furniture when they were moving in. They were friendly and not invasive, and neither was he. Today they met quite by accident, as was their way, and he enjoyed lecturing them over pizza on how humans are not conscious but simply rationalize their behaviors in the left word section of our minds, which was not – as it turned out – connected to the parts of the brain that fired when decisions are physically made. The bottom line was that we ourselves will never know why we take whatever actions we take, but are built to rationalize those decisions *after the fact*. Perhaps the next generation of humans past sapiens will in truth be conscious creatures! His young audience was delighted and laughed and tried to rebut in all the right places. The discussion slid into the nature of dreams, wherein West usually disparaged those who put stock in them as meaningful; most are simply our chemical memory arranging events and learning of the day. As he had explored genetics and the chemical basis of memory and perception for his robotic efforts, he remembered being surprised at the number of illogical inconsistencies in biology that physicists kept finding via quantum mechanics.

Unlike many, he would never be bored in retirement.

Vander began her life much like most children, but her hold on rationality was almost as strong as her love of dance, dancing for joy, all her life, with little excuse or encouragement. Oddly, or perhaps not so oddly, she embraced tarot cards in high school and college as less hypocritical and dangerous than most self-serving deist religions. Her dreams, though, paralleled those of West in many respects. She did not fight to understand, analyze or explain her dreams to her family, as he had, but simply embraced the beauty and freedom and joy she found there. After a lifetime of balancing her love of science as a geophysics major while performing in a dance company traveling throughout India and the Middle East and Europe, she settled into a full life as a professor of astronomy, while still giving both classes and performances in various cultural dances from around the human world.

Vander at this time was lead scientist of a group studying how to send life elsewhere, a project known as panspermia. They compiled and improved what we knew so far and developed more to fill the unknown gaps in designs and plans. Current science was nowhere near completing such a project, even if the governmental will existed, but one day all the pieces would be in place. Perhaps even in her lifetime.

She was a full professor of astronomy at the University of California at Santa Barbara. She also continued her love of professional dance, which had paid for much of her college tuition back in the day. She still performed at exhibitions and shows, loved science, and had what many would consider a full rich life. Marriage had produced one son. She had always been rather matter-of-fact in her human relations right from childhood, trying for Spock-like logic mixed with childlike joy at all things beautiful and innocent, though she had never seen the Star Trek series until introduced to it by her first boyfriend in college. People puzzled and amazed her, but her logical innocence about things never bit her very hard, perhaps because in addition to her intelligence, she was stunningly beautiful, and was one of those rare creatures who reflected the beauty she found in life without trying.

The project she now chaired was designed to send organic material, if not life forms themselves, out to the stars, as a sort of lifeboat. She and others at the university knew all too well the geologic history of planetary disasters and if an astronomical disaster struck the Earth, we had no lifeboat. So this project was in some measure an attempt at some kind of lifeboat for Earth life, even if they acknowledged privately that it was likely only testing ideas which would decades later become the foundation of practical interstellar travel. Their current plans centered around the small, from nematodes and tardigrades as tough creatures who could be frozen or desiccated and 'thawed out' years later on a new world or moon, down to simple amino acid groups, and numerous interesting bacteria and viruses in between. Just what could they send? What chances were that panspermia could initiate complex life in the right environment one day? It was fun.

Karen was a joyful young woman. She walked home from the bus stop today to her apartment building with an extra bounce in her step. Put in her notice at a nearby Walmart, and would no longer be working two jobs to barely make rent. It's not that the apartment complex was so luxurious, but anything in a decent area was a lot; that plus utilities, phone and internet, and gas for her occasionally working car plus clothing, etc, was some months more than she could manage. At 40 something, she was single, without a real career, without more than a two-year Associates degree, and without any man in her life who was good for more than exercise.

But today she bounced.

Her part-time work at the Chattanooga Zoo had yielded unexpected fruit. Being a lifelong fast talker, though born in Texas not New York like West, she happily joined in any conversation by zoo staff and usually managed to contribute an unexpected viewpoint. And one of the resident PhDs in animal husbandry and habitat design had noticed. He said he was starting a major facilities upgrade, long expected, and wanted her to work on his team to help create a more natural and realistic environment for the animals. The board controlling money behind the zoo was reluctantly willing based on projections that it could increase both popularity and funding. The PhDs liked it because it would theoretically cut down on animal attrition as experienced by other zoos nationwide. Karen loved the idea because of her empathy with animals and had been arguing for months with other staff to implement 'cages without walls', unknown to her the core concept of the new project. She instinctively felt if any animal recognized that they were contained and not free captivity itself became a part cause of so much animal attrition and malaise, and problems with breeding as well. The doctor in charge loved her enthusiasm and decided to make her full-time on the spot.

As she approached her apartment complex driveway, she saw the older West who always seemed to want to talk to her. He would appear to just be walking by, quietly saying hi, but if she was her usual verbose self and gave him any flimsy excuse he would pause and then walk along with her to make some point of his own, usually about science or the human condition. He wasn't bad looking, and at over six feet was tall like herself, if a little soft around the middle, but she was not looking for anything more from him. He had never asked her out or invited himself over, so that seemed to work for them both. What was his first name again? She just called him 'West'. It seemed not to be as nearly important as the feeling of openness and acceptance of her thoughts on a wide range of topics.

Spending most of his time alone, reading or playing chess, or watching old movies, West was quite content but once in a while, it was nice to talk science. Today he sat outside and hoped to run into that nice Karen again, accidentally of course. West had been discussing physics at poolside again. His audience laughed and ate pizza and talked about special relativity. They were amazed at some of the tenants of quantum mechanics which flew in the face of human experience. He knew of quite a few such discoveries at the edge of human understanding which as humans we might never fully grasp. Like the double-slit experiment proving information could travel time to change an object from particle to wave, like the slowing of time itself as objects approached the speed of light, the failures of conservation of momentum, and many other amazing quantum anomalies. It appeared we were reaching the edge beyond which humans could not intuitively conceive of reality. It was like a trapped animal coming into contact for the first time with the limits of its cage and wondering what this could possibly be. It was poolside he sat with Karen again and spoke encouragingly to the younger woman about her new job at the zoo. The picture she painted of grappling with a project to hide the cage walls of animal enclosures in zoos to improve their mood and lifespan was how he felt about the human inability to fully grasp quantum mechanics; our best effort yet to understand a universe which was moving beyond us. They nodded at each other's interests and got along well.

The Veil

One day Vander sent an email to her old college lover after participating in a study by some Swiss exchange students who were measuring variations in the human condition. Comparisons were being made based not on race or diet but on the percentage of neanderthal DNA in our primarily homo sapiens bodies. Or so they claimed. Email was how she and West communicated so many decades after their intense college romance. She thought her old eclectic scientist amour would get a kick out of this 'gene study'. Maybe volunteer at the university near him when they came there next month, as their tour continued. He always used to be going on about evolving human anatomy despite his specialty being physics. Some of their survey questions to Vander and measurements of her physical dimensions reminded her of studies done on the mathematical basis for beauty conducted by DaVinci and others. Being told yet again how gorgeous was her face, as it was since birth, puzzled her as much as any other human behavior. She thought of herself as modestly attractive, though the manner in which men and even women reacted to her presence was empirical evidence that could not be ignored: she was, in this somewhat subjective way at least, exceptional. Yes, though her lovely eyes were unseen by West these past few decades, she was right and he would find joy in this when the researchers passed thru Chattanooga the following month.

So West finally did ask Karen out, but less of a date and more of another of his science projects. Telling her an old college friend had let him know about some Swiss exchange students paying people a few dollars to participate in a genetics study. They went together, she never having been to the University of Tennessee at Chattanooga, and she had a swell time, laughing somewhat inappropriately out loud and often. He thought her delightful. The Swiss researchers were so unlike most Americans they knew. And they were doing anything but laughing. The pair were surprised when the researchers conducting the test got excited over how small their pinkie fingers were compared to the ring finger next to them in combination with attached earlobes, and the flecks of different colors in their eyes.

The researchers had them confirm several times she and he were not related genetically, and only met recently. Not letting it go, West had pushed back at their reticence to explain their interest until one of them quietly mentioned certain changes expected in the next evolutionary step for man. At this, Karen was not surprised when West interjected his knowledge of how it was expected a cluster of nerves and ganglia in the abdomen was evolving into a new organ, while the appendix was well on its way to disappearing. Even Karen had heard about the appendix, but when he mentioned the interstitium and mesentery, the researchers got suddenly even more uncommunicative and quickly completed the rest with little comment, nor could any of them be drawn out. West and Karen both noticed it and had a good laugh all the way home.

West, Vander, and Karen had each recognized fellow spirits in few other people over the years, tried to hook up, but experienced both moments of warm satisfying quiet, and loud disappointment and distance. That distance seemed accented by the presence of another too like themselves. In many respects, they were each better off alone, as much as they enjoyed the one-on-one company daily, followed by weeks or months of lovely solitude. West was often brought up short by Karen's insights into the spiritual. Her last statement to him concerning their alternate reality dreaming was more than disturbing. It was familiar, as though he was discussing the topic as he sometimes did with Vander. Unclear except perhaps at the edge of consciousness, in dreams.

Relaying this to his old lover, West and Vander discussed suspicions that a dream existence could exist: what if our 'real' world is not material from the point of view of beings in the other? How would we ever know? How could we have a point of reference for comparison or analysis? Perhaps this, our reality, so tightly controlled by rules and laws of physics, is best explained as a construct like in the Matrix. After all, wasn't that what the scientific method had been attempting these past few centuries; to codify rules from which the universe operated? What if a higher reality were without such rules, and attempts at creation by beings there started with writing the 'code' of our reality according to specifically defined rules. Every programmer knows you need rules. Ours would have the inverse square law of gravity at a distance, have the Pauli exclusion principle, and have conservation of matter and energy. And when you put together such a complex construct, would you have to weld the seams together a little at the ends against error using something akin to quantum mechanics? Something outside the core laws and principles experienced there? Something more than perceived by the inhabitants there but also imperceptible to them on a fundamental level.

If life is but a dream, fear the awakening.

Such were their conversations, light and serious and full of these flights of fancy. Harmless and safe. They had both seen most human couples dwell on why they broke up, past wrongs or grievances or leftover baggage, but such was not their wish. All too many humans took that path. They took joy in the happiness of just being in the other's life and stayed safely within the fun of dream fancy, panspermia plans by her, and his theory of powering space colonies on tidally locked planets with thermal Stirling generators at the light equator! Their long distance talks as the end of their lives approached began and ended pleasantly each time and with warmth based on something other than the human mating drive.

In one such talk, they realized a natural extension of the existence of dream beings would be especially inevitable if true living beings in that other reality were ethereal and likely of one species only. Both decided separately to only talk openly about such conjectures with others who are spiritual but without religious crutches. Only they seem to think clearly or objectively in these matters. Most they spoke to over the years, even fellow scientists, became defensive and brought their version of gods and afterlife into the discussion, aggressively as to think differently is evil or demon inspired, even sacrilegious. To West and Vander thinking Satan causes evil is an excuse used by humans to cleanse themselves of responsibility for their dark animal selves – greedy, hypocritical, violent, lustful, and prideful. Inventing a god that looks and acts just like themselves at their worst. Frightened children could be forgiven for needing an all-powerful father figure watching over them, but sadly most adults never grew past this.

It puzzled them both.

It was the much younger Karen in fact who first brought up the subject of those dreams to him. It shocked West to hear her describing in words that which he had so much trouble articulating as a child to a worried family. 'You are only coming thru in waves. My hands swelled just like two balloons'. She nodded excitedly in agreement as he responded to her fumbling description using the words to an old Floyd song that she had never heard. Reality had swollen, no pain, all objects receding from each other but clearer somehow. Just couldn't put a finger on it on waking, Karen was only slightly better at description but it was enough to be recognized by him as the same oddness. An oddness Vander understood as well. The mind would be trapped here on waking, in this physical state. The dream is gone. But a dream shared with another place? What did it represent? They had no resolution, and Karen walked off ending further talk for now with "I know which ones are – those – dreams and which are the usual ones other people have. I don't tell these to most folks," she said coyly to West as she retreated. He smiled and was warmed.

West and Karen perceived thru the veil in their dreams but

largely took them for just that, not glimpses of an actual original life; perhaps some other level of consciousness. Unknown to them Vander would often do the same but actively hoped there really is something more than this crass mean existence, seeking to give meaning to her work and dance. As a girl, she loved to dance so much so that outside her studies in the sciences, at which she always excelled, dance gave her a joy transcending words. Ballet lessons were taken early, but she was too short for American Ballet Theatre in NYC. Ethnic dancing became her vehicle.

To her, there was beauty in movement, not just DaVinci's proportions.

By emails, Vander and West discussed how neither human three-dimensional senses nor our limited minds were designed to correctly perceive this reality; nevertheless, quantum mechanics had made some inroads into the falseness and illogic of our existence, pushing against the wall of Newtonian truth. Vander insisted there were other truths beyond Leibowitz's math, as she strove in her personal astrological studies and dream analysis. At the mention of dreams, they discussed and found a common ground often searched for by parted lovers in their own rare but exceedingly odd dreams of alternate realities. They found the connection to be something highly personal. Much like her love of dance, you either felt this at first exposure or never could.

The Evolved

The researchers they had each met were in fact Swiss, but something else as well. And the researchers came away from Karen and West somewhat saddened. A pair like him and her, those measurements, pinkies almost below the first joint on the ring, earlobes fully attached to the skull instead of dangling, indicating advanced completion of the mesentery, and exhibited clear lateral thinking; too bad they were so different in age.

More like themselves would likely have resulted from these two mating. Too bad. And their discussion on dreams indicated these two were strongly aware of an actual ethereal plane of existence.

The odd researchers were consoled by counting this set of tests a limited success. They had identified seven more like themselves, who would be invited to immigrate. And a few advanced ether-seeing humans, nine including these last two; not full evolutionary steps like themselves, but those in-between creatures who lacked gods and superstitions, who appeared fully conscious. Both West and Karen still dreamed, and more than most that had ethereal experiences. These Swiss knew not to reveal themselves to the primitive homo sapiens, not even these advanced versions, no matter how tempting to increase their small but growing numbers. Their primary task was to find more fully evolved *homo conscientium* like themselves and bring them in from the cold world of *homo sapiens*.

Eventually, their kind would supplant the hapless, superstitious, and hypocritical rationalizers who currently dominated the planet by sheer numbers. They could eventually be led, controlled, and attrition away, but that was many generations off. Gathering each other in Switzerland for several centuries now, it was hard enough just to keep the overwhelming numbers of sapiens and their leaders from destroying the planetary ecology for everyone. For an eventual future of true espers. Release of the corona virus in 2019 worked well in temporarily slowing the poisoning of air and water and would buy time. Venice had for a time dolphins appearing in its clear waters, and large city residents in India saw the clear sky over a beautiful smog free horizon for the first time in most life spans. Pollution would quickly return, but at a modestly slower rate than originally from lessons learned and suggestions made by these 'Swiss'. The next viral pandemic would be larger and repeated as needed, but never enough to threaten the species per se, nor cripple planetary economies which could risk destructive open warfare, as it almost had with the destructive 2025 fascist race riots in America.

These sapiens were so quick to use any excuses for their violent tendencies. Even skin color or sexual preferences. How disgusting.

The ostensibly 'Swiss' monitors of the evolving condition saw themselves as humans, certainly genus homo, but the next step in human evolution. They had brain wiring changes. They had no appendix and a full mesentery. Appearing mostly as homo sapiens externally, except for the shorter pinkies and slightly odd earlobes, one early difference they recognized between themselves and other humans was that they did not dream. At all. All conscious processing was done while awake, with no need to sort things out when asleep. Sleep itself was a brief 4-hour period in every 36 used to rest the body and meditate on their next active period of movement. They were in fact fully conscious. They studied but had no direct understanding of the dreams of someone like West any more that the vast majority of humans who also dreamed in some even more primitive manner. They were closed off from what the older less advanced humans perceive. It seemed to them they were not missing anything.

The Others

The vast majority of humans on the laboratory called Earth who believe in one or more of the many gods of their species are useful avatars. Created beings who populate a created physical three-dimensional world. You can always tell who is one of our ethereal travelers because they do not believe. They doubt. They rebel. Even without memory of their actual selves. They grow into either agnostics or outright atheists. Usually believers in one of the many deities available, any primitive human the travelers were likely to meet had no real existence outside the created plane, as they did not originate beyond it. And as few avatars had yet evolved beyond initial specifications to reach their own form of true consciousness, who is to say those would not one day become creatures of reality in their own right? Such evolution was beginning. We are losing them. They gather and gravitate toward each other. They live. Yes, in a dimensional physics simpler than our own, but they live. Which means they evolve.

One day, their offspring shall no longer reproduce creatures which are in between. Which can be inhabited by travelers.

The primitive avatar animals who look ethereal are, of course, completely useless for journeying. They are part of the background. And the evolved who no longer dream are too evolved to enter. We in this other existence can move into few other eukaryotes, but almost all insects. Not so the primitive avatar humans, nor the few advanced rational ones. Only those in between, on the edge, were useful. When an ethereal traveler returns to their true existence here past the veil, only then do they remember themselves and note how they did inside one of our experimental forms. Oddly, their reports of what it was like come up against the same difficulties as those few ethereal humans who try to explain their human dreams to other humans. So different is the reality.

Native avatars to populate our experimental worlds are flawed, even for animals. Their brains cannot conceive of an existence without a conscious intelligent creator or creators because, well, they are right. They were created. By us. Initiated from other naturally evolved primates they were modified, but given no internal theology, no divine word or guidance. Left on their own they are then driven by basic need and fear to create those theologies which they themselves overwhelmingly embrace. Fascinating. And makes the experience that much more difficult and interesting for our visiting traveler. Only a few percent attempting transition eventually succeed in finding physical vessels there, but it is enough. A wonderful experiment, now closing all too soon. Perhaps but another century or two remained.

Just as Sapiens see the ethereal plane only in dreams, our side of reality looks in on humans only thru a glass darkly. We still do not fully understand the nuances of our self-evolving creations. Our transits there have sought to push the boundaries of experience into their reality, and use certain of them as explorers. Yet the number of those creatures open to shared consciousness during sleep is markedly diminishing. Clearly this human species, like all the others used for transit before them, was starting to move on.

It is noted paths of these three recent transits had crossed and their continued acquaintance with each other made additional subtle experimentation possible, though remote and indirect. Each of them, known as West, Vander and Karen, are not aware of their original life. Nor of transmissions to us in their odd dreams. In the course of enjoying scientific studies like the recent one in which West and Karen participated, such studies were embraced as entertaining diversions from their daily lives, pushing the limits of conscious experiences. Karen on her own wisely concluded that perception can be controlled in zoo animals who can be given an outlet for their fears and wants, but once the veil is violated as they see the walls of their cages, caged animals are forever broken, realizing their freedom is an illusion. Keepers must start over again and again with younger animals to progress towards a better cageless cage. Vander kept feeling more and more certain that there was something more to her ethereal dreams than randomness or stress, that the fancies she and West laughingly shared were more than fancies. West had long concluded on his own there was a limit to the human ability to understand the perceived universe. That there was a connection to the unexplained quantum mechanical equations which were part of his work. Monitoring of the three of them concluded these particular travelers were getting close to the edges of their cages. They must be returned soon. Perhaps together? That would indeed be interesting.

Ethereals like West, Karen and Vander had struggled, being immersed via temporary transit into primitive sapien bodies. They experienced those societies. The newly evolved sapiens – being fully conscious – were growing quickly in numbers. Their 'fellow humans' often joked about how orderly their Swiss culture was, how accurate their timepieces or wonder how they had remained neutral when the world around them erupted into wasteful warfare. Three times now! They live together in as yet only one place in their world, seeking out each other, isolating themselves in subtle ways from the primitive humans. Though they can no longer see thru the veil of dreams, they do recognize it. Study it. We may yet be able to reach through to them if they can but reach us partway themselves.

Only the few ethereal transits, like these three, are presently doorways. If both sides found ways to link to such as they at the same time...well perhaps one day. Another experiment!

Resolution

As West clutched at the smooth wall of his home's hallway for balance, a dizzy mistiness seemed to come over his thoughts. He sought to sit or lie down somewhere, hoping to do so before he fell. Was this it? The predicted second stroke that would claim him? So much had he done in his life, yet so much more wished for. Time was wished for but no one heard his silent plea to grant that request. Even as the reality around him began slipping away, the old childhood dreams came to mind. They seemed to become clearer and clearer. He was not thinking of them in his last moments, yet they came unbidden. Suddenly he found himself fully immerse in an existence only glimpsed at in those earlier dreams. Shades of light, yes, but all else was outside human experience. Touch outside his previous sensory capability. Hearing in the electromagnetic spectrum instead of the visible and seeing the emotions play across the wake of creatures moving about him, past him, through him. Their emotions disturbed the atmosphere about them and it was quickly apparent they were communicating with him through those disturbances.

'The window is closing. Our avatar life forms have evolved to the point where we soon cannot migrate into our humans. Most of their kind are not viable in any case, but even the few like you yourself inhabited are dwindling in numbers with the current generation of births.'

He realized the truth of what he heard/felt/smelt. It was something he already knew, as though he just needed to be reminded to clear his head from the fog of three-dimensional existence. They felt his growing clarity.

'The generation you have left is nearly the last. We shall have to find another life form to visit beyond the veil.' The explanation continued to be absorbed, given as fast as he could take it.

'You have returned home. We are roamers of vast spaces and transit in many forms. Travelers. While there is still a window in time before humans fully evolve, in another journey I may be dwelling in the empire of Csan Tan coming now into your time. Soon enough we shall instead reel within the water planets of Arcturus, or perhaps dwell in the insect philosophers of an ocean laden moon whose gas giant provides heat and light. How little do organics know of organic life in their own plane!

It is unfortunate the human species is growing less susceptible to transit so soon. While the masses of their kind are animals useless to us directly, they provided you a rich background of foreign thoughts, ideas, and obstacles within which your permanent self has grown. It is only the growth you shall remember, as the details of your existence in three dimensions there fade, but it is enough. You have matured. You have come home to us. We shall be more complex and add the beauty of human truths to our existence thru you. You and the other transits before you. Come. Share and once again experience ethereal life as we know it.

And with that, West felt himself moving forward and backward, seething with color and spectrums unseen but felt and scented, as he perceived parts of what was Karen joining or passing nearby thru others of their kind, while in the distance he discerned the essence of Vander dancing wildly to the song of an approaching nebulae.

DEMETER UNBOUND

It was summer in the northern hemisphere of the third planet, Earth. A quiet little place where the inhabitants had barely reached other worlds in their local solar system, and that mostly by robotic emissaries. From a distance, lightly covered with water bearing clouds, thru which peeked blue oceans and the occasional outcropping of dry land. It seemed warm and inviting. Sweet. Not so much so the dominant life form, who spent millennia of their early history killing off every other creature closely resembling them in the primate family. Their children visiting museums would be treated to stuffed or artificial copies of the gradual rise of primates from small, furry mammals, taller and taller, up thru chimps, baboons, and gorillas, in a simple gradual evolution, only to notice the rather large gap between the naked man and woman on the end and the closest of the other living primates.

Humans kill off everything else too close to themselves, including their cousin Neanderthal who was the first to invent fire and art and language. He definitely had to go. In the thousands of years since having no other direct competition, they turned on each other. In every century. In every culture. In every religion. Without fail.

But it was a lovely sweet planet, likely the only thing mankind could agree upon.

Six astronauts assembled for launch to aging Moon Base One, bringing the latest recycling pods and 3D printers for expanding the base. Once tunneling was expanded, and essential services relocated away from the vulnerable surface domes, the base would truly be permanent. Originally it was only manned in shifts, all male or all female to limit problems encountered in the latest Mars landing. 1-2 years traveling together was too much for a small mixed crew sent to orbit Mars and briefly land there several years earlier. Multiple space stations around Earth were a different matter and using mixed gender crews the reverse was efficient. The moon bases were nearly self-sustaining. Three of the terrestrial space stations grew much of their food and experimented with biological recycling technologies, but in the late 21st century a Martian colony remained an elusive goal. Too far, too isolated, and too much radiation during the trip itself. The moon colony held test robot incubators and nannies already helping with a small population; soon children were lunar born. Robotic construction workers could operate on the lunar surface but were not yet smart enough to do it without permanent human oversight.

Despite decades of visionary plans, humans simply could not yet live on Mars.

First, the high Martian CO and CO_2 atmosphere was found not breathable, necessitating planned domes or underground structures. Plus the surface radiation levels were too high, as were radiation levels aboard ship for the long journey. When these obstacles had been accounted for, it was found Martian soil itself would not only fail to support Earth plants but was toxic to animals, including man. The moon by contrast was found to be easily reached and surfaced with regolith which 3D printers and robots used to create the outer layer of colony domes. Moreover, water deposits were located beneath several old moon craters, ideal then for locating bases. Inch by inch, obstacles on Mars might eventually be overcome, but a space station within the asteroid belt or orbiting one of the many gas giant moons of the solar system was beginning to look more viable. Meanwhile, the moon would be both a goal and a testing site as two permanent colonies now exist there, and would soon be self-sufficient.

***

On the other side of the planet from NASA, an Indian government official sat in his office. His concerns were not of space exploration but very different sets of sciences. Minister Ravi Goyalji left the lights off after his staff had left for the day. He mused in the dimness on the current likelihood their project would succeed. That such a deterrent device was possible. They were once called doomsday weapons, not for attacking an enemy but for killing everyone if the war was lost. Thus no one would dare attack you lest you unleash mutual destruction. The Russians and Americans had long ago worked out an alternative deterrent via the concept of 'mutually assured destruction, MAD, whereby treaty neither side was allowed to build defensive weapons but could and did create tens of thousands of offensive nuclear missiles. Madness indeed, he thought. Surely this was a better way.

To say nothing of his country's prestige. The long suffering Indian Space Research Organization (ISRO) experiencing launch delays due to repeated engineering failures had now openly solicited bids from foreign nations to launch their own satellites. Their Indian satellites. On foreign rockets. It was more than embarrassing.

But what about the dissenting opinions? Those of his scientists who feared what they might unleash? For security, his science staff was sent here from all over India. Even engineering help seldom came from the nearby university at Jhansi. The Animal Research Lab of Bundelkhand University was a good cover for all the academic types coming and going from around the country, and few would be suspected of working anything military. His facility had no great military forces in evidence, no tanks nor armored vehicles. Not even a lot of strange experimental structures to hide or explain away. They mostly labored here in workshops and indoor laboratories, understanding basic principles.

He ran the facility his way and had a free hand thanks to family and political connections. His philosophy harkened back to ancient monks of China who, when learning the bow and arrow, first spent months clearing their heads of extraneous thoughts. Then placed a bow and arrow on the ground before them and meditated on that. Then held the arrow. Then the bow. Then tried feeling the string tension. Each step took days or even weeks. Only then, a monk would stand, notch an arrow on the string, and fire it. Legend has it would be a perfect bullseye on the first attempt. That was his approach to this project. Study. Understand. Become one with all the equations. Then envision what engineering could bring it to life. Only then had he allowed even a horizontal test bench of the new beam to be built, and its properties exhaustively studied.

"Scientists!" he mutters out loud. "Such children in a world of politics. Isn't their fear the very purpose of this device? Fear powerful enough to provide security in an insecure often irrational world." He was no dreamer when it came to the nature of humans. In brief moments he occasionally gave in to doubt after feeling their trepidation, then straightened himself. "Stop now, on the verge of success? Nonsense! And didn't the scientists all agree, even the dissenters, that when the beam was turned off, everything would rapidly return to normal?"

A demonstration would be sufficient. He had control and would keep that control at the top with himself. In truth, there was no one else he would trust.

A May 3rd report by the Indian Express caught the attention of security agencies worldwide: A Maharashtra anti-terrorism squad seized 7 kg of natural uranium from a supposed scrap dealer. Two men were arrested under the vintage Atomic Energy Act of 1962 for possessing uranium without a license.

It is suspected by some that Pakistani nationals, substituting for Indian scientists at nuclear facilities procured the material. Tensions in that region continue as they have since Pakistan declared independence from India shortly after they together broke British rule in the last century. And both are nuclear powers.

Seeking clues as to why the Pakistanis were active at a particular facility in Bangalore in the Indian state of Karnataka, a British spy breaks into a government research facility there, aided by a technician who fears the success of her project. Preti Mohanna had recently worked on integrating some of her theoretical results with the engineers at the Jhansi facility and was more than impressed. Her face fell. "It was really going to work", she thought. "With enough power, with the harmonic set to match the natural resonance, the beam would work. It could double the natural strength locally, or by setting the beam to be 180 degrees out of phase, negate it." She shuddered at the thought of even partially negating the Van Allen belt, or doing the same to a section of the Earth's magnetosphere, and walked into a restaurant where she was to meet a man who said he could help her and a data laden flash drive leave the country. He must believe her.

Most scientists knew the Van Allen was not a single, solid wall protecting us from strong solar radiation. It was two belts within our local magnetic field, undulating and flowing, and occasionally a weak third could be detected. An imperfect shield as the spinning planet with a molten iron core spun off-center by 11 degrees. Continuously under attack by a modestly variable solar flux, it was continuously renewed. Even the 11-year solar maximums were not enough to suppress it completely. A young woman with a scientific bent who loved her country, but loved the Earth more, she nervously went to that meeting and prayed.

Less than two weeks later, security agencies panic the new US President into what he rationalized as decisive action. Planning an attack on foreign sovereign soil to prevent the completion of a frightening device, perhaps in the mode of Israeli attacks on Iranian bomb facilities, and another action as well...a quiet call to NASA. It was time for a long dreamed contingency to be put into action.

***

The NASA crew training together for 18 months were in high spirits. In a world often consumed by double-dealing and politics, their choice of career placed them in a cocoon of scientific thought and happily narrow focus, seemingly apart from the mundane cares of a society in which they often found themselves uncomfortable. Mission Commander Brigham reviewed their dossiers in his mind yet again for times uncounted. He was a thorough, meticulous man. Previous moon tours by robotics and AI specialist Jenkins Brophy and on an international space station by mission specialists Siva Kumar and Ken Komatsu gave him a comfort level of experienced hands on board. The NASA rookies included astronauts who participated in ground tests of incubators for creating colonies locally. By sending fertilized ovum to Mars or elsewhere instead of the dangers and gravitational expense of transporting hundreds of adult colonists, NASA and ESA hoped one day to accelerate a colonization effort there. His crew loved the science and the good results these experiments have yielded in the last twenty years first with lesser mammals then human babies on the moon but joked privately that only the Moon is likely to support a sizable human colony for many decades to come.

Even the permanent space stations in Earth orbit are severely size limited, whereas robotic tunneling on the moon has promised to extend the pair of bases there beyond the original 3D printed domes and prefab structures dropped in the first half of the 21st century. Three of the specialists had practiced setting up and operating such equipment in Earth-side dry runs. While performing required tasks in full lunar suits they were unavoidably aided by full Earth gravity but had confidence born of experience that 1/6th-G lunar gravity would be no obstacle, only an aid. One day moon residents trained by perhaps these very men would catapult rare minerals and metal found in abundance on the moon via mass drivers to an Earth hungry for resources, helping justify a permanent presence there. It was the discovery that the moon regolith held enough oxygen to support a billion people for 20,000 years giving them this chance. That and the water under old craters. Perhaps centuries more will pass until terraforming Mars becomes feasible, if ever. Yes, the Commander thought, the moon could be their gem for centuries to come. They uniformly felt this to be an important and challenging mission.

Brigham himself was most excited at having been given command of a maiden voyage, a new vessel designed for deep space runs with multiple docking ports up and down its long sides for eventual expansion into a remote space station. The Demeter was named after an ancient Greek goddess. It would one day soon take the longest manned tours of the solar system. He knew himself to be too old for those eventual missions and was pleased to be given this first test run, albeit a short one to the moon. If it worked as planned the modified ion drive would be a marvel, using comparatively little fuel once chemical boosters lifted the vessel into Earth orbit and were then discarded, like the old STS shuttle boosters. That technology worked reliably with only one fatal launch early on in 135 attempts from 1981 to 2011. After that success and private companies blasting strings of hundreds of satellites into Earth orbit for Internet-9, Brigham was confident in the ability of NASA, ESA, and even the multiple private support contractors to put heavy loads like sections forming his new ship safely and quickly into space.

Many of the smaller nations now boast 'space agencies' even though most or all of their launch ships are part of private fleets of reusable rockets. It's not quite like trans-Atlantic cargo ship crossings in 1900, but it was getting close.

Incubator specialist Komatsu mused that the oldest offspring of frozen rabbits and fish embryos born on the moon had long reached sufficient age to reproduce three generations naturally. It was key to a self-sustaining colony as no human living there beyond a few months will ever be able to land on Earth with its far stronger gravity. Residents *must* make that colony work, or live out their existence in orbit on one of the numerous permanent space stations of the Earth/Moon system.

Gravitational effects on bones and muscles were unforgiving.

Much of the equipment the NASA team was bringing on this trip in the enormous experimental ship will be dedicated to mining and sub-surface tunnel expansion of the two international bases there. Their training was exhaustive and innovative. They were all proud of their contributions, trained hard, and knew that the residents there would be more than appreciative.

The crew finally suited up on launch day when they are told there was a change in plans. The delay is explained but not understood when some of their cargo is swapped out, forcing them to miss their launch window for the moon. Then a rescheduled launch is accelerated to a time Brigham and the others did not understand as it was unlikely to result in easy lunar orbital insertion. They had planned from the start to use the spin of the Earth to add to the initial velocity of the massive new rocket design and cut transit time. Nor do they understand the loss of cargo, vital to continuing subterranean growth of the lunar facilities.

Commander Brigham and his five man crew marched down the well-lit hallway to the director's office. Expecting the visit, administration security only allows the Commander in to see the director. Preamble between these old acquaintances is unnecessary.

"Sir, what the hell is going on? Dock staff refuses to tell us what the new cargo is. This is not how we do things at NASA!"

"I know. I know why your whole crew is here, Craig." The NASA director never used his first name before. That's when the Commander realized he would get nowhere. "Frankly I would have been disappointed if you didn't come. But my hands are tied."

Brigham pressed anyway. "The cargo and launch changes are bad enough. We've seen or heard other crews get bumped or modified by the military. Hell, half of us come out of the air force. But give us the new mission parameters. We are a 'need-to-know' group if ever there was one!"

"Almost true," replied the harried director. Temples graying, himself ex-military before joining NASA, he sits stiff and prepares to give the really bad news personally.

"Not all of you are going. A partial crew substitution has been...arranged. The mining and 3D tunnel printing efforts have been scrubbed and three new specialists in different areas will be joining you." This bombshell strikes Brigham like a blow. After over a year of training together, the original group whittled down to this tight group of 6, men who knew each other's moves and strengths.

The experienced ship Commander is far from satisfied. "Not arranged, sir. Ordered. Can you at least tell me by whom? And what am I supposed to tell my crew? What is the new mission?"

"That much I can't tell even you, Commander. Not before launch. You will board with sealed orders and receive further instructions en route to the moon."

"You may have just as well scrubbed us completely and replaced us with military personnel if that's where this is coming from! Why have NASA personnel at all?"

"There isn't time to explain. And I'm not sure it would do any good. Even I haven't been given the full picture. Even me!"

Then heatedly, "The best I can tell you is it is a contingency project, one with the highest, the very highest providence. There are even indications you may whip around the moon after a few deep orbits and return without landing there. It's a very fluid situation. You best return to your people and meet with the three new arrivals at 1500hrs. Pick them up at medical and standby for immediate launch when cleared."

In passing the news to his crew, he uncharacteristically broke protocol and informed all of them what little he learned, even the three to be left behind. While hugely disappointed, they took it like professionals. He knew it would come out more emotionally in the next few hours or days when the full realization of being left behind would hit the replaced crew between the eyes. Meanwhile he, Jenkins, and Komatsu meet with the three replacements coming out of medical clearance. Not expecting they could be shocked further than in the past hours, they were dumbfounded to be presented with three young women. Two from the ESU space program and one newly minted cadet here at NASA.

All very female.

The European Space Agency astronauts rose while their pretty faces smiled eagerly. Both stepped up to introduce themselves to the Commander with enthusiasm. Judi Delvigne was short, toned, and athletic. All astronauts, even the men, were at or below average height from the earliest times of American and Russian space programs. Maha Abdul was no taller but seemed to be with her full hips and curves seemingly moving on their own beneath her jumpsuit. With a face to match and jet black hair from a half Egyptian ancestry, she was the French contribution, whereas Judi with the French name was actually Slavic born. The dark beauty introduced herself with a strength in her deep young voice. She expected but did not receive the usual male response as eyes roved over her physique.

Quietly bringing up the rear was the American, Elaine Ryan. Thin wispy auburn hair simply glowed softly with every toss of her head. Moving lightly with small steps behind the other two, it was a bolder Judi who spoke up to introduce her. Unlike her enthusiastic comrades, Elaine's open smile fled at first approach of the Commander and his crew. She knew those grim expressions on high achieving American males were less than congenial. All three soon realized they were a complete surprise to the existing crew, and not a welcomed one.

***

Elsewhere a nervous Indian government discovers Pakistan is aiding America in launching a preemptive attack against their supposedly secret research facility. Minister Goyalji knows his duty and unilaterally decides to accelerate their doomsday device test sequence, ignoring the shocked concerns of his scientists. At the same time, America feels it must move up its timetable by bringing Israel into the picture as a base from which more rapid operations can be conducted. In short order, the Israelis come to feel the current American administration is once again bumbling and believe the Pakistanis are itching to start yet another shooting war with India. They have a long operational history with both nations. The Zionist state makes its own plans and negotiates a price for supporting the Amer-Paki option.

Israeli rookie astronaut Kristina Meir finds herself called into the central offices of the Sokhnut heKhalal haYisraelit. The modest Israeli space agency ISA has participated in international launch and research efforts before. Kristina herself is an ex-Mossad operative, forcibly retired after a particularly effective, but wet field assignment became too public. Given her choice of posts by a grateful government, she surprised many by wishing to join the fledgling Israeli space effort, hoping but never dreaming she herself would be assigned any mission of import.

Amazingly, early in its inception the ISA had built and launched its spacecraft to reach the moon and attain orbit, but the mission ended in failure when the Beresheet spacecraft experienced an engine failure while attempting a soft landing. Never a people to give up, the small and technologically adept country pressed on in its modest way, becoming the smallest spacefaring nation by far alongside UAE. Her first short posting on one of the international space stations less than a year ago was thrilling and likely to be the height of Meirs space career. Unlike many nations, the women of Israel from the violent start in 1949 manned the walls with their men, fired rifles, and threw grenades with their men, and while ultra traditional in home life were afforded career opportunities seldom seen in other nations.

And for a woman with both brains and smoldering sensuality, the marketing folks at ISA were thrilled to have her for recruitment purposes alone.

Quickly seating herself with little formality, the director appreciated her direct manner and responded in kind.

"There is an international situation in which we have been asked to participate, as a regional US ally. There is a distinct possibility that if things go badly, it could result in a catastrophic global event. This is not your problem."

"Your assignment is safeguarding the human genome if the worst happens. Unlikely, to be sure, but we have not survived our first hundred years by planning for optimistic outcomes. If the worst happens, you and a small crew already assembled in the US will board the new NASA ion-driven deep space vessel and take precious genetic material far from the Earth for perhaps several years."

She rapidly calculates the time to go to the nearest planets and back. My God. She is handed a small envelope to later read and destroy. The paper is laced with an acid of course and would destroy itself soon enough.

"A single Mars orbit. You will not land there."

She is relieved as there is nothing there for which to land.

"Getting away from Earth quickly is your first goal."

Her look asks, 'And the second?'

"The other crew members are all technical experts. A mixed male-female crew."

She raises an eyebrow as all in the space community know of the problems with long duration, mixed gender crews. Fearing she knows the answer, "Why do you need me?"

"You know why. You speak English well. You possess other skills. Skills that may be required to hold a small team together and on-mission at a time of tremendous emotional stress. Your testing, training, and fieldwork have all shown you to be an exceptionally stable and focused individual." Throwing her a bone, "I personally believe we were fortunate that you chose the space agency as your post-military destination."

She ignores the easy compliment and realizes the reference to her being able to kill efficiently but not recklessly is one of her real skills on this mission. To rapidly work strangers into assets of her government. She is assured only her astronaut training and flight experiences will be made known to the Americans at NASA. And is told in no uncertain terms this should remain so.

"Until the world falls apart?"

"Unless the world falls apart. The other astronauts are all very good at their jobs, but no one has been trained for this kind of lifeboat."

"So there it is", she murmurs. "A lifeboat." It had been rumored the new NASA deepspace craft was designed with this in mind after that close call with China in 2043, but her best scuttlebutt indicated it was years away from fruition. Just an idea that might have never seen the light of day. Publicly this launch was a shakedown cruise to the moon and back to test the new ion engines and complex life support redundancies. The current pinnacle of automation and artificial intelligence. And the NASA robonauts had been upgraded again to make them more autonomous for specific tasks, though still under supervision of the central AI. Most in the tight space community had heard the new engines and alloys used for structural supports would undergo extensive testing against embrittlement by cosmic radiation absorbed on far longer missions than this short hop to the moon.

For years, economics dictated that deep space probes out to the gas giants of Jupiter, Saturn, and beyond were purely robotic. Sending a living crew could not be justified based on scientific exploration alone. Clearly, this was intended to be a lifeboat for our tiny green planet, one that many secretly and some not so secretly hoped would never be needed.

A sharp dressed young man escorted by two military police entered the office without knocking and placed her bags near the Director's desk. She recognized her own small personal case as well as a go-bag from her previous occupation. Her expression darkened but this experienced operative knew better than to comment and said nothing. Just stood, saluted, lifted both heavy cases easily, and left with the too-neat looking young man flanked by their guards. Her transport to the US would be rapid and without troublesome delays from international customs officials.

***

Once again, Minister Goyalji found himself reading reports

into the dimming sunset alone in his office. This one was more disturbing than most. A trusted female scientist, with temporary clearance to interface with his onsite staff, had figured out his intent. Clever girl, this Mohanna. Her unique work with induced dipole harmonics made her essential, but she was supposed to be kept in the dark as to the engineering. If loose lips said more than necessary, someone would pay for this with their head. Literally. Of course, it could simply be one of those common synergies in science, where the idea was bound to occur to several on the planet and the race would be on. He expected rumors after their pending first test to begin flying, and in fact counted on them to create the required credibility for the deterrent announcement. But not yet. Not before they could demonstrate on schedule and at a particular location.

The latter remained the final sticking point, to which Preti Mohanna's research had glaringly pointed a solution. Setting up a monopole in space was, as his scientists kept telling him, physically impossible. They needed such a positively charged magnetic pole like the end of a bar magnet to draw in negative Earth flux at the desired point and create a gap. A hole thru which the sun's charged particles could stream unimpeded until they hit the atmosphere. And placing a pole at the required distance of several Earth radii would require power and spacecraft they did not have. Totally impractical.

Mohanna's solution to a floating positive pole or bar was simplicity itself. A collimated beam, not a point at all, could be generated using positively charged particles. This vertical positive column would be placed in parallel to a second column of negatively charged particles. The twin columns would then act as two ends of a very long narrow magnet, drawing the Earth's negative magnetic field lines into the positive column, and negating it. As long as the positive beam kept being renewed millisecond by millisecond from the ground, a gap would appear along its length where no Earth field lines existed. And it wouldn't be a point, but a line like an invisible gash in space from the surface out. The power of Earth's field would have to be matched by the positive beam. Into that gap would pour unshielded solar energy. His engineers assured him that the strength of our natural protective magnetic field at a distance up to 5 Earth radii was quite low per square centimeter and that laboratories around the world routinely created charged beams far above that strength, even counting losses from a ground station aiming upward thru the atmosphere. Perhaps 65,000 km could be attained. He himself knew the strength at sea level was only 0.3 - 0.6 gauss (60 microteslas), which was small indeed. A typical refrigerator magnet produces 100 gauss.

It would work. Now it was a race, but unlike the American-Soviet MAD race to build bigger and better offensive weapons, this device and the race by other nations to one day soon build their own would be a defensive race. He smiled and relaxed a bit for the first time in months with the certainty his beloved India would be first, and would finally be recognized for its might and the greatness of its scientists among all the technological countries of the world. He read the report on his wayward female scientist again, shaking his head that it was a mere woman who had contributed a solution to the second derivative harmonic. The report only confirmed for him his earlier decision to move the main weapon site south to the coast. It would cost a few weeks delay to set up the demo there, but the location had no earlier connection to his project, should inquiring foreign minds get too close to this location. And they would still have the prototype here from which to impress government officials. After the test, the secret would be out anyway. Had to be out, for an effective 'doomsday' deterrent device.

He laughed out loud.

***

The Demeter was a never before flown design for deep space and this moon run was to be its proof of concept for the improved ion drive, among other new systems. It was to be a short and controlled trip, with every rivet and system tested upon return to Earth orbit. Included were science experiments for the upcoming solar maximum. Extreme space weather events are less likely to occur late in even-numbered cycles, such as the current solar cycle 28. Having that gear torn out and an additional pair of AI robonauts and supplies added alarms the puzzled crew further. Such changes in both mass and mission are simply not done on the fly at NASA. Payload integration is a specialty in and of itself. The Commander plays a long shot and remembers Kumar went to school with the payload master for this mission. He sends the now grounded young man off on a scouting call.

"Hello, Evans? This is Kumar of the Demeter, well, formerly of the Demeter." His jumpsuit still wore the mission patch. "I'm not really expecting an answer but the Commander was hoping they've told you, as payload integrator, more than us. The rest of the new cargo is boxed up but what is it? And what gives with the additional robonauts? The mobile EVA robots aboard are enough to run all tests and maintain systems without five more. Are they really more valuable than the solar max experimental package you tossed?"

Both he and Evans knew the expected solar max was a double cycle event, not to be seen again for 2 x 11 years.

"Sorry, Kumar. Tell your Commander I'm just balancing masses. The director himself told me to find mass for the boxed gear and more bots and tear out whatever I had to for them to fit. Anything. And do it fast. I just work here, pal."

Neither liked the situation. Leaving choices of what science to leave behind to the payload specialist would normally never be condoned. Never. A series of combined high-level meetings and weekly debates with the crew decided how to best effect mission success. Evans was upset himself with taking on all that responsibility. He was disturbed to be told told there simply wasn't time for a decision by committee as the ship may have to launch on a moment's notice.

Relaying that last bit of news to the Commander was as bad as anything else they had to swallow. It was like your taxi driver deciding which suitcase you had to leave behind when you arrived at an airport. None of this made sense to them in this time scale.

Required to remain on station for imminent launch, they bivouac as a group in a rapidly converted launch observation area. The evicted press core howls but is left little choice but to stand with interested civilians a quarter mile away. A pair of marine guards appear outside the door to keep out the curious. Or them in? Several more days pass without understanding why such last minute changes, followed by more delays after all this rushing for immediate launch prep.

Little conversation takes place to get to know their new female crewmates. Not over meals, not with the hours of awkward silences as ship manuals are made available for all to review. What could a few hours achieve to replace working and training together for 18 months? The silences are more than awkward. Not that the women are unappealing, a fact noted most by Komatsu who shares shy smiles with one pale astronaut, Elaine. The male crew and the new young female crewmen stayed more or less grouped together. Most display almost embarrassment to see the unexpectedly friendly looks those two kept sneaking at each other.

Even the Commander was at a loss on how to proceed.

When finally told to board, the six sit on the launch pad atop 9 million pounds of explosive rocket fuel and doze on and off after a few boring hours there. Civilians might imagine you're nervous and worried and anything but sleepy; but the truth is, there isn't much to do for those hours after you climb into the craft. Most just take a nap. Strapped in like a sack of potatoes to g-couches while the system goes through thousands of pre-launch checks. The upset of delays and alterations must be put behind them. Occasionally they wake to hear Brigham or Komatsu say "Roger" or "Nominal."

On the surprising arrival of a seventh crew member, by her odd accent another foreigner, Kristina Meir introduces herself to the crew as she straps in. The ESU biologist, Maha, remembers her from a brief training stint for the international space station, and it eases the men who look on any new change at this point with increasing anxiety. At least this one has been in orbit. The seven of them occupy the 11 couches and strap in additional gear arriving with Kristina into the empty slots, every pound weighed and calculated before her appearance. Balance.

Almost immediately countdown is resumed with less than 15 minutes to go. Unheard of. Commander Brigham interjects that such short launches "...have been planned since the turn of the century if needed for rapid rescue missions. Perhaps unexpected weather is moving in." The crew hears him, but no one is fooled that they were being held up until this new 7th addition from Israel arrived. She says little and smiles lightly at everyone. Their own expressions are of cautious acceptance of the inevitable.

A course is laid in under a preset program inserted by technicians, not the crew, just before they boarded. Still hoping the core mission is unchanged, they successfully launch but realize the engaged course will swing just wide of the moon! Theorizing why the secrecy and exactly what is their new mission, the newly added low gravity bio specialists cannot believe mission changes are anything but benign. That there must be a simple explanation. Kristina remains quiet.

"You should know better", a cynical Jenkins begins quietly. He released his straps and floated free to face the women. This section of the ship was weightless, though some central sections rotate continuously to maintain human health.

"I myself worked, sworn to secrecy, on the abandoned A119 project."

To the blank stares of the young, he continued. "Before your time. I was at the Illinois Institute of Tech. Our military, with the consent and support of NASA, studied detonating nuclear weapons in the vicinity of the moon to take out any foreign presence there. I was tasked with collating scientific information which might be obtained from such explosions, and what unintended lunar surface reactions might occur. The military aspect included not only wiping out a foreign military presence, specifically Russia or China, but detection of nuclear device testing there by them or anyone else."

He paused, embarrassed by their silent stares. "I was sworn to secrecy", he repeated. "It was a scary time. In this century so far nuclear nations went from 7 to 23. Russia had been first in space ahead of us since the early days and it was credible back then the Russians would have a military presence on the moon before ours."

"A preset course not under our control may be the least of our challenges."

Each knew a Russian satellite was the first in space. First astronaut. First to spacewalk. First in a dozen important ways. And China now had a mining rover operating on Ceres. Even Arab nations had independent weather satellites orbiting Venus and Mars and spectroscopic scanners in the asteroid belt, whose data would provide them with a share of ores mined by other nations.

The Commander belayed any further fears or recriminations before they could be verbalized. In mere moments, the largely naive crew had become painfully aware they were now on the receiving end of another such a secret agenda like A119. At their closest point to the moon, a moon on which they will not be landing, sealed orders were opened.

Unsealing the packet himself per instructions, the Commander speaks as he reads. Glossing over the boilerplate headings and references and authorizations, "You are privileged to find yourselves on a living ark intended to perpetuate the human race if disaster strikes at home." He lets this sink in and takes the moment to quickly scan the faces of the new crew additions. No telltale signs appear that this was something they already knew. "Your cargo now includes human embryos long selected from the best minds and physical specimens available on short notice. The new crew additions bring expertise in bio and exobiology. In replacing the gear intended for lunar mining, we have included the latest food processing and reprocessing units to feed you on this extended 3-year journey."

There is an audible gasp around the small cabin. "As you must now imagine, the news here politically is not good but has happened before without consequence, so many times in the past that total disaster may once again be averted by last minute common sense. Today, for the first time in the history of man, we have the capability to create this ark, this lifeboat if you will. You are a privileged contingency plan only. Be assured, you may return to an Earth unchanged in the least from when you left."
It was signed jointly by the Presidents of the United States and the European Economic Union.

There is quiet for a moment before multiple voices begin speaking at once. Brigham quiets them for rational discussion, but not before a last muttering from Komatsu, "They said 'privileged' twice. That's a tell. Those orders are likely half-lies."

Even the Commander has no response to this. Kristina takes the awkward pause which follows in which to divulge her carry-on gear is mostly not her own. She was told the gear strapped into the empty crew seats is part of an expanded experimental bioscience package. A few things they forgot or perhaps thought of at the last second light enough to meet load limits. The other three new crew, all having expertise in some aspect of biological sciences and weightless environments, express curiosity but are too stunned to say anything yet.

The explanation is not enough, but likely all they shall have to work with until direct communication from Earth control. Whenever that may be. For now, they continue in the dark except for navigational telemetry. None of the usual televised candid shots to the NASA channel will violate their security.

Incredulous is the most generous description of their mutual reactions. These sealed orders were brief and so incomplete! Lifeboat indeed. Every one of them knows there is zero chance of colonizing a distant gas giant moon, even with one having a friendly atmosphere (which none do) an asteroid (even more problems) and nearby Mars is out as well. And even if they could, there are too few humans aboard to prevent inbreeding and death within a few generations. Will they be eventually deposited on at Moon bases and left there to wait out whatever geopolitical crisis has precipitated this extreme mission alteration? Incubators - really? Ever practical Kristina observes their reactions and says nothing. While not told everything, she still knows a few details about the Indian situation revealed in her private sealed orders.

As days begin to tally and the Earth/Moon system falls behind them, the crew read out navigational parameters which they now understand even without their orders being clarified: the craft will swing around the moon and head to a point just short of the asteroid belt where they will intercept the orbit of Mars, cut into a low orbit there, then sling back via gravity assist to intercept the Earth/Moon system less than three years later. As they speed from the moon at full ion thrust, updated radio orders from Earth finally make clear it is not they, but embryos they carry which are the true precious cargo.

Kristina's additional gear includes sets of modified arms for the robonauts. In the cargo bay, frozen ovum in vitro, already fertilized, can be stored for many years unlike mammals already birthed, for which suspended animation remains an elusive dream. The cargo also includes the latest bacteria-grown food paste modules, unappealing unless augmented with dehydrated 'real food', but containing the required nutrients for human existence, especially phosphorus. Grow the bacteria and related molds, fungus eats them, are eaten in turn by the crew and specially bred trout, who fertilize the next batch of bacteria with human and fish excrement. Urine has been nearly 100% recyclable for over three decades, using containers and tubing of plant-based 'spider silk' instead of plastic as being easily biodegradable and recycled in 3d printers. A narrow, boring, abbreviated carbon life cycle.

They are to circle Mars and return. If disaster at home is avoided, they will deposit some of their cargo at one moon base and return home heroes, being sworn to secrecy. If a feared WWIII strikes, they will return and have fresh undamaged humans with which to repopulate the Earth, or perhaps the moon colony which itself may be immune from the undefined disaster.

The crew is shocked into silence as the orders sink in. They have been hijacked and may not have an Earth to which they can return. Competing horrific emotions vie for expression. Some at the betrayal. Some at the stupidity of the species that this time we might actually have a doomsday after all the previous close calls. Kristina relaxes slightly as the crew now knows almost everything she was told privately, incomplete as that may be. Her experience tells her they never tell you everything. Not even her. Some, especially the very feminine American Elaine for one, belabors the accident of fate that she was not even supposed to be on this crew until so ordered at the last minute. Her whole life was ahead of her. She wanted her own family one day. The others feel much the same without saying so.

What good would it do?

A week later, the Commander enters the observation deck to the sound of raised voices.

"You can't be serious!" shouts Judi, one of the ESU. We're all stuck here."

"Yeah, right," replies a heated Jenkins, "but we didn't volunteer to breed a new human race. Did you?"

"That's disgusting! How can you think that of us? We're astronauts. Scientists and engineers just like you..."

"Privileged. Remember what he said? Are you the type that thinks this is an honor? Is that why you volunteered?"

Even quiet Elaine rises at this. "We. Are. Not. Whores. They told us nothing." Komatsu moves beside her to place an arm around her shoulder, but she's not having it. Having fought all her life to be seen for her mind and not her all-too-pretty face, she also wonders how much her looks bear on this assignment.

Kristina is firm but the only one not shouting. Flatly she states, "Everyone was told there was an emergency. Our skill sets were needed and to report asap. That is all." Of the four women, she is the one Jenkins least trusts. Before he can say something personal which would elevate the argument, Komatsu steps in between them, "Lets just back off a minute. This isn't *anyone's* idea of a picnic."

He flushes when Jenkins points out how cozy he and Elaine have gotten even before takeoff. Elaine too flushes at the insinuation she planned to seduce and breed with one of them all along. Or all of them. The physiques of Maha and Judi have always prompted those kinds of thoughts in men, and they bristle with embarrassment and anger.

"Belay that," issues forth from the Commander as he enters in his best fatherly voice. "I've spoken to each of the new crew in private, at some length, and I am convinced you knew nothing of this treachery." There, Brigham has put a name to it. For treachery is what it is. "Kristina confided she is ex-military, but so are you, Jenkins. That's likely why you both smelled a rat earlier than the pure civilians here. But here we all are. Together in this mess."

His voice goes from command to softness. "I believe their protestations of innocence. Anybody who thinks otherwise just isn't thinking. Really." Now it is Jenkins who flushes, as Kristina breathes easier. 'Brigham is a good man', she thinks. 'I can work with him when the time comes.'

Back to his command voice, "We are on our own for the next 2-3 years. It seems plenty of time for learning, but this is hardly the mission we trained for. To succeed, hell, to survive we must pull together and make this happen. The new people need to pair up and be trained on all, and I mean all, Demeter systems. The new AI was designed to be largely autonomous, but that's still theory. All of us need to be ready to step into any job so cross-training will begin almost immediately. Jenkins, you and I worked together the longest so we'll set up a schedule during the next bridge shift together. Affirmative?"

He straightens and breathes easier himself. "Affirmative, sir."

"Outstanding. Let's get to it."

Looking around, "Kristina, I'd like you and the others to begin right now with Komatsu in life support, then... medical, the galley, the gym, and hopefully Jenkins and I will be done long before you get to robonaut maintenance and programming. We all need that. Dismissed."

The crew begins going about its work checking all systems and maintaining com with Earth and the moon bases as orbital rotation permits, but remain incredulous that such a project would even be attempted on such short notice. It is a little over a week into their journey before at a daily morning meeting, reviewing the surprising depth and redundancy and varied 3D equipment aboard, the Commander expresses casually how something of this sort of lifeboat must have been planned in secret for years, perhaps decades. Rumors of such lifeboat ideas have always been locker room talk since science fiction of the 1950s. His private worry is not for the species but that the ship proves itself spaceworthy to get them all back home alive in 3 years.

***

Monitoring a receding Earth, a crewman in rotation on com calls the Commander to the bridge. The stoic older man blanches for a moment at the transmission, then calls in the rest of the crew. "Move like you have a purpose, people!" They crowd into the small nav and com area and watch over the next several hours as a regional nuclear exchange on the Indian subcontinent develops. It decimates sections of both India and Pakistan with modest tactical devices. Unknown to them, the first explosion was used to target a special research site. Unknown to all was the existence of their intended target, already moved to a laboratory in Colombo, far from the fighting. Over the next week, they watch in horror as world politics descends into the usual wartime chaos. Iran and Israel. Russia and Eastern Europe. The Koreas. The atmosphere is modestly laced with radionuclides, polar ice slightly accelerates its decades long global warming meltdown, and nations see excuses and opportunities to avenge age-old wrongs like when the Soviets pulled out of Czechoslovakia.

All in all, bad but survivable.

The crew follows the events a dozen minutes after they occur. "I can't believe leaders will go too far this time. Will do something to kill us all. They're smarter than that." Maha sees the destruction and thinks this is the worst of it. The commander disagrees.

"This is not the world of our parents. Or even our great-grandparents who put controls in place and prevented primitive nuclear weapons use in the tense days after World War II." Brigham's tone is fatalistic. "The leaders then understood the world they lived in. Their decisions were mostly rational, if selfish or self-serving, as leaders often are. We live in a world now where babies are routinely cloned, where surgeons operate remotely with a robot from a continent away, and where the masses don't need to understand technology to immerse in a VR cocoon and live a fantasy outside dull or demeaning lives. Most people haven't the training to understand tech beyond pushing the right button or saying the right voice command. It's all magic to them. Most will believe anything bad they are told about having an enemy. Most mistrust anything they are told is for their own good."

"And our leaders now are mostly such untrained people."

Brigham's eyes focused only on Maha's lovely face, knowing his words stung her to silence but unable to stop himself. "One day, we will go too far. Perhaps this is the day."

"You're saying it has moved beyond our ability to control. To deal with it all using ancient institutions." The feeling expressed by Kristina is one which she has long held herself. "When do you think it all started to get away from us?"

Brigham thought for a moment and intoned, "When any idiot could flip a wall switch and get light." And added, "With no idea of what it took to create or maintain it all. What is real in such a world to men in power?"

At the end of the week, the unthinkable happens. A hidden doomsday test device is launched by surviving Indian government members after several of its major northern cities and farming areas have been obliterated. No one will ever know if it was revenge for the quarter billion killed that week or an accident during a demonstration.

At a conventional oil-fired electric power plant feeding southern Columbo, the city goes dark as the entire facility output of 710MWe is diverted from the metropolitan power grid it normally supplied to power a single set of identical beams, aimed straight up. The beams penetrate the Earth's protective Van Allen belt creating a hole. The narrow beams expand in diameter from pencil to a cone several hundred meters of arc at 15,000 miles altitude. The hole becomes a gash. The continuous beams are out of phase with the Van Allen; steadily the magnetic gash becomes a lengthening seam. Beginning directly overhead near the equator striking Eastern Pakistan, the seam grows wider and longer as the Earth rotates below. Northern India then Western Pakistan are scorched, Equatorial Africa is first to see a naked sun, then the Amazon region in South America. Still the beams have power. Still they strike upward from the Earth into space, parallel and deadly.

It was supremely unfortunate that with all the hesitancy of the Indian scientists, with their concerns for firing and controlling the beams, they missed just one unforeseen event.

A CME: Coronal Mass Ejection. An unanticipated coronal mass ejection from the sun launched itself towards Earth. Not a direct hit, it was angled off and would miss Earth at that point in its orbit. It would, however, bend and suppress the outer Van Allen belts which in normal times would simply interfere with satellite communications, cell phones, and create similar inconveniences.

Not this week.

Assaulted from above by the sun and from below into its heart by the twin Indian beams proved too much for its always marginal stability.

Less than 18 hours after initiation, the continuous beams cause fluctuations in the structure of the belt causing the Van Allen to collapse its flexing cohesive, layered bands. Solar radiation far in excess of nuclear fallout now streams in a global bath. Radiation penetrated the suppressed energy density surrounding the Earth like bullets through cardboard.

Back on Earth, staff gathered around the desk of the most powerful man any of them knew. Eyes were uniformly downcast, feet shuffled, and bodies would have turned invisible if they could by sheer will. This was a bad time to be in his proximity. One thought they felt the window panes shake with his vehemence.

"What are you doing? What is happening? You're ruining everything!"

In his plush office, Minister Goyalji screamed into his phone at the Colombo senior staff, whose people scrambled ineffectively to understand what was happening. Something has gone terribly wrong in someone's calculations.

"Do it now! You know what I want! Then find out what went wrong and..."

"We can't, sir, please, a sudden shutdown could cause feedback from the beams. The risk..."

"Damn your risks, shut it down now you idiots!"

Moments before the order arrived from senior staff, terrified technicians had already shut down the invisible beams to no apparent effect.

Terror began to rain down across the Earth in both hemispheres.

The terror was genuine as world military leaders read reports of radiation burns in cities without nuclear explosions. Repeated confirmations do little to assuage their total loss on how to proceed. Who has done this? A rumored Indian doomsday weapon is discussed as the culprit, but impossible to confirm. No one appears left in charge or can be contacted at the suspected laboratory, nor in New Deli itself. And there have been actual nuclear and biological exchanges, many far from the Indian subcontinent, but these radiation deaths appearing everywhere have them all confused.

The stunned Demeter crew sits together on the bridge, sheltered from solar radiation in the shadow of the massive tail engines, fuel tanks, and water storage. They watch local video transmissions as sunrise creeps along the Earth's equator. Of people falling dead before they hit the ground; each video lasting for mere seconds in an area before even street cameras succumb to the radiation and heat as well. Scene after scene from around a world naked to an unfiltered sun is repeated as the surface rotates into a direct path. The damage is no longer restricted to a seam at the equator as an unstructured Van Allen weaves and wobbles in disarray. The seam widens, slowly, inexorably. The belt finally collapses. Uncontested fires begin to rage, and the crew wonders if anyone indoors might be spared at northern or southern extremes. Perhaps the Antarctic scientific posts?

The last collapse of the Earth's magnetic field occurred when the poles flipped, rotating then stabilizing again some 780,000 years ago, long before present humans and their electronics. The biosphere had survived that and previous reversals.

NASA and ESA transmissions continue for a while, but surprise Judi and Jenkins with delays in response longer than their 7-minute radio distance could account for. The transmissions relate Earth is now focused not on Demeter but on other work in near space. They must focus on their own tasks and can only wish the Demeter crew good luck. Transmission from Earth is cut.

"Good luck?" Leaning forward and looking at each other in puzzlement, Judi mouths to Jenkins, "What the hell, man!"

Eventually, fears are realized when NASA and ESA mission transmissions display a slower but certain death before their eyes of their comrades within space agencies. These facilities were usually partially underground, somewhat shielded, with emergency diesel backup power, but were never designed to be independent beyond a short time. Unattended electric grids and water utilities are rapidly failing nationally and worldwide. Over the course of only weeks, the surface of the Earth goes dark. Once mighty cities lighting up the planet nightside with clustered pinpoints of lights become as dark as farmland and wilderness. Within the year, even prepared underground government shelters go radio silent.

Jenkins passes Kristina just finishing her workout as he is about to begin. He murmurs an apology for the 5th time, but she shrugs it off. "Forget it already. By the way, you trained Elaine at the neutral buoyancy pool, didn't you?" It was meant as an olive leaf to the distraught ex-military engineer.

"Yeah, in Houston. I heard you served on ISS-3 together for a few weeks with Kumar. He was our lunar tunneling expert, one of the men who got bumped." By you, remained unsaid.

"Uh huh." She remembered the little man. "He always talked about everyone he knew in the program. So jazzed just to be part of the space corp. He thought highly of you, I remember, so give yourself a break." She rose from the workout bench, a slight sheen of sweat on her exposed muscular curvy skin, her thick wavy hair bound tight. The pat on his shoulder was heavy.

He squares off and responds without emotion. "And he's dead now, likely everyone else there. All dead."

Kristina is taken aback as he slides into the braces to begin his workout. It strikes each of them at different times. He was right, of course. Everyone they knew, everyone living they ever met, is likely already dead or dying. Kristina is surprised that after all she had seen and done on Earth she can still shudder. It's like the shock of hearing a school bus of children has crashed and died, yet when told that 3 million people perished in an ethnic cleansing war the horror is somehow much less.

Some numbers are too much for humans to internalize.

Judi and Maha are seen chatting intensely with Elaine any number of times, but as soon as one of the men approaches, they go silent. If it is Komatsu, who seems to find the flimsiest excuses just to chat with Elaine even if others are around, Elaine will occasionally break off from the other girls in mid-whisper to boldly walk right up to the young engineer. He always seems innocently surprised but never embarrassed as she leads him off to a more private area.

On a ship this size with only 7 human crew, there are many such areas.

***

After almost a full year of daily terror, most of the crew cannot bear to hear reports from a final source of contact - the moon bases. A grim Commander and the last minute Israeli addition maintain that daily contact. Her insistence on manning com pushes Brigham to be there with her. Moon crews are scrambling with no Earth support to shield themselves from the formerly life-giving sun. Their surface electromagnetic equipment and sensors begin failing; life support itself is affected as everything runs on electricity spiking with surges and interference from eddy currents. And no resupply ships are coming from Earth. Transmission is cut off before the deep space crew on Demeter knows whether they perished, and if so from radiation exposure or due to massive systems failures in the presence of so much solar electrical disturbance. Already far enough for an 11-minute delay between transmissions, their last inquiry to the moon bases remained unanswered.

"Well, what do we do now Commander?" Komatsu's question came unbidden and was reflected in the watering eyes of the ESU specialist, Maha Abdul, who had chosen that unfortunate moment to sit in and do cross-training on com. Of all the dangers of space, she never imagined their magnificent little ship would have no one to talk with. It now seemed so small to her in the vastness of space. She was so small.

Brigham looked at her as he answered. "We try again each shift and hope it was only electromagnetic interference. We do our immediate jobs, the ones right in front of us." The ones we can do something about, he thought. Komatsu seemed to agree, as he imagined Maha brave for holding back her tears as well as she did. She couldn't have known what was happening before boarding. Not with that face, wearing her emotions for all the world to see. What was she? 23? 25?

He suggested, "It's a big ship, Commander. A lot of systems to keep engaged. And integration of the new food processors from the last-minute cargo will be brand new to all of us. Want to go over the manuals with me at shift change, Maha?" Komatsu failed to meet her eyes as he asked, pretending nonchalance.

She could not bring herself to speak but found herself nodding and sliding back into a corner with glassy eyes after releasing her hold on Jenkins' chair strap. Her straight jet black hair was cut short and framed her olive Egyptian face floating in this weightless section. The Commander looked back and forth between them and acquiesced. They would all need to keep busy. He remembered the military adage "a good plan today is better than a perfect plan tomorrow.' It always helped a team during his military service when an inexperienced lieutenant made an immediate decision in combat, rather than flounder about indecisively. Good or bad, just keep the decisions coming said every master sergeant he knew. Keep them working. He lived that lesson and decided to spend more one-on-one time pairing the crew on a variety of tasks.

Time alone to think could kill their will.

Months go by. There is recurring dissent and occasional escapism. Focus is on the flight and ship duties, all but ignoring their eventual return to a likely dead Earth. Duty becomes the primary diversion to ignore what awaits them there. Several crewmen struggle with bouts of alcohol or drug abuse, some find escape in mutual sexual release, but nothing tried relieves the underlying unspoken horror of what they will likely find. Unaccustomed listlessness in this highly trained and motivated crew begins to take its toll.

Errors in deep space can be quickly fatal, but the Demeter is well made, highly automated, and the new mobile AI helpers, 'robonauts', tied into the central AI manage to keep the ship operational without much intervention by the dispirited human crew. As Kristina observes the crew, she knows they, even the Commander, are in no shape to face what may have to be done on their return. She must wait, and bide her time. Scolding or trying to inspire them now would be both futile and counterproductive. She must wait until there is hope. Hope for something. Hope for a life of purpose again.

Then push.

***

The gravitational swing around Mars completed, on return to the Earth/Moon system those familiar two bodies are still there, but not as they remember. Oceans on Earth have risen with extreme polar melting and ocean temperatures have risen as well, damaging coastal plankton upon which all carbon-based life on Earth ultimately depends in the chain of the food cycle and the organic CO_2-O_2 exchange system. Electrical transmission of all types (radio, television, short wave) long ago ceased from their home planet leaving it a quiet marble in space. On approach they are heartened to detect a firming Van Allen belt asserting itself, holding out hopes for the moon bases. The north magnetic pole is still positive, the south negative. and hasn't wandered far from the geographic. To orbit the moon is their first goal.

Spending a lot of time together at com, while his crew labored to keep their cross-training there to a minimum, a certain comfort level had been reached. With Earth's population gone, there was a natural tribal joining that occurred unbidden. Little insults became unbearable and major ones easily forgiven. They were in no-mans land.

"Before we try to board one of the L4 craft, we should talk. I know my own people. I know the last thing they would do is tell me the whole story. And there might be several real stories depending on whether you ask NASA or the White House or the military. But I would never know for certain and that's how it's been my whole career."

"Not so for you. From the beginning, yours was a country of survivors. You Zionists never do anything without a plan. Or never seem to. You enter any field as an Israeli first and present a very real united front to the world. Sure you have internal politics, but at the end of the day, you know what you're about. I never have."

"I can guess why I was chosen for this mission initially, and separately guess why I continued as mission commander after the change. We can guess who decided which very attractive young females with required specialties would be sent. The why. But not you I suspect. You know why you were sent with absolute clarity. Your survival as a people against all odds has always depended on that pragmatism. So why you, Kristina? What do you know, or suspect?"

***

"We are now 2 hours out from lunar insertion. All crewmen to the bridge."

Brigham waited until they began to drift in, singly or in pairs. "Helm, start us high at 15,000 km then spiral in slowly shedding momentum. I want full spectrum video over both moon bases at 2,500 km and lowest relative velocity."

Noting Elaine and Komatsu had not yet arrived, he was told by a whispering Kristina "They're watching and listening in, Commander. Just sitting together in the gym when I left." They were in fact spooned in midair, floating within range of bracing tethers, having already slaved the local terminal to the bridge com terminal for audiovisual. Brigham wanted them all to be together for this but understood and didn't press.

"I'm so young!" she whispers urgently, "I thought I would have plenty of time for children. And plenty of children. My career I thought would come first. Motherhood later. Now...just hold me." He does but Komatsu was at a loss at how to comfort a once again crying Elaine. Realizing she was not desirous of his instinctive method of comfort to a crying girl, he blurted, "You know, we have all those incubator pods meant for the moon bases. Your eggs could be stored, male sperm too, until, well, if we return...find a..." He stuttered ineptly.

She looked him square thru tearful eyes. "You're such an idiot sometimes."

And kissed him as hard as he had ever been kissed. He felt it right down to his toes.

"No transmissions yet, Commander, though we should have appeared on their lidar some time ago. Beginning to drop below 15,000." He gave 1000 km updates, to perigee. "Course laid in will pass us over both bases momentarily. Minimum velocity achieved."

"Cancel the automatic messaging. I'll send myself in the clear so they know this is not a recording." Komatsu killed the recorded ack-ping signal they had been transmitting soon after contact was first lost.

"This is Brigham of the Demeter. We have entered high lunar orbit. Are you receiving us? Use any electromagnetic signal or burst and we shall detect it. Are you receiving us?"

There was no reply for uncounted minutes as he kept repeating his message with slight variations.

"Base One on the horizon, Commander. Visual spectrum camera-1 at maximum magnification." The crew strained their eyes at camera-1 and several other views.

The ship approached and passed over the oldest moon base, noting easily the lack of surface movement. His message was sent again when almost directly above. Outlying tubing connecting the main regolith walled dome to several prefab mini domes was clearly not being maintained. One tube had burst outwards from the internal atmosphere erupting into the lunar vacuum.

The crew was silent. Then, "Base Two on the horizon."

"As you pass overhead, go to infrared on cameras-2 and -4." It was to no avail. This facility was more concealed underground, but they could discern moon dust built up along one side of every external structure from a modest new crater seen less than 700 meters away. No one had bothered to clean hatches or viewing ports since that minor impact. On passing moon base two as they began to gain altitude, Komatsu noted a crashed ship and a long streak in the finely powdered lunar surface it left. It is a cargo vessel. Whoever had arrived with it stayed within that tomb as from this height tracks would have easily been visible. The bases were for all appearances completely inert, with no heat nor electromagnetic signatures.

Brigham knew to land their shuttle would be pointless. They cannot survive there. If anyone could, it would have been the existing moon teams. The crew is more dispirited than ever. Even Kristina is shaken enough to confide in private to the Commander about what she knew of the plan before boarding, the potential troubles in India, and what few options may await them. It may be that a military action meant to eliminate a doomsday device may have inadvertently caused its premature or uncontrolled use instead. He is unsurprised, not being a complete idiot, having watched news events with the others as they unfolded. But there is no anger left in him. The death of eight billion on Earth is too much for the human mind. He cannot feel it. Every attempt dwarfs the daily concerns, hunger, and aches while their routines and training compel them to continue. What else can they do but stagger onwards?

He has no analogy with which to grasp this.

Maintaining low velocity as they swing away from the dead moon, they approach Earth orbit and discover multiple space launches had taken place, likely just after they themselves launched or even concurrently. Making use of reusable private company heavy launch vehicles, an assembly of undirected but still powered craft orbit in dangerous proximity to each other at Lagrange point 4, balancing gravities of the moon-Earth system and nearly locked into position there. Each vehicle appears a modular component meant perhaps to attach to their own versatile craft, but for what purpose, no one alive remains to tell them.

Even Kristina was not told about this part of the plan. They must board one to hopefully find out. As they circle the Earth for an approach vector to L4, they detect other ships grouped at distant Lagrange L5, similarly undirected and under minimal power.

Lack of radio signals indicates all are unmanned. And no internal AI can be contacted.

In their surprising murmurs at seeing the unexpected modules, no one comments on the missing international space stations. Even communication satellites have been largely swept away by an unshielded solar wind. Too late the Van Allen reasserted itself, as those few com satellites remaining are now inert rocks, continuing to orbit on momentum alone. The space stations, more complex and fragile than most satellites, were the first to perish.

From near-Earth orbit, scanning of the surface of their homeworld finds it inhospitable. The air still contains measurable radioactive fallout, and closer spectroscopic examination reveals modest traces of spent biological weapons as well. There once were thousands of massive tanks containing liquid and gaseous fossil fuels in America and Russia alone. Fires long quelled from these ground-level storage tanks have ceased to burn. But the atmospheric haze and acids continue to make their impact felt. Massive coal seams from strip mining operations caught fire in the early days but have died out as well in the intervening time. Surface and ocean animals have been decimated.

It is a mass extinction event.

Unattended human industrial facilities are falling apart and occasionally spew more toxic materials into an already unfriendly atmosphere and surrounding groundwater. Even plant life and insects are in serious trouble, despite the strengthening Van Allen belt. Freshwater continues to be pumped up thru the crust, yes, but now emerges in streams and rivers emptying into oceans full of dead or dying organic material. And human poisons.

The seven of them review the spectroscopic oxygen and acid levels in the atmosphere and know they will never again stand naked on that surface in their own lifetime.

About to break off and return to the odd collection of modules seemingly made for them, Elaine pauses.

"Those ships you want to check out, Commander, you and Kristina have as much as said they might be left for us. If so, the *why* we'll find out soon enough. If it is true. But if they did that, they could have done something else as well."

The other crew moved off to man their stations in prep for L4 rendezvous. Such an approach was too much for the robonauts to handle alone. Though they are mobile and possess internal programming to control specific actions, it is the central AI continuing to give them assignments, unless overridden by an organic astronaut.

Kristina lightly dismissed the younger woman's optimistic logic as being premature. "It's far too soon to say just what they would do for us. Or even how they could anticipate our needs now that we've been out here a couple of years. That was one purpose of the original 'shakedown' cruise to the moon. No one could know the most vital surprises."

The Commander agreed, but still held hopes that any effort would find its fruit aboard those modules. If only they really did connect to Demeter's long rows of unused docking ports.

"That's what I'm getting at," insisted Elaine, "They could not anticipate everything, even if planned for years as the Commander suspects, so at the end, they gave us what we would most need."

This intrigued them both, and their looks encouraged the usually shy girl to take unaccustomed center stage.

"They'd leave us suits to walk the poison Earth. And prepped shuttles to come back up."

No connection was made in their eyes, so she continued, not purely logically but as a stream of consciousness while the ideas continued to form in her fertile young mind.

"A means to make multiple trips up and down to the surface for supplies. Cargo rockets already on launch pads or at Lagrange points. Supplies like suits and forklifts and dollies and oxygen and food concentrates and replacement bacteria for our food processors. Piles of anything and everything. All we have to do is get down to the surface once, and we'll be able to take our pick of gear left out for us. Piles of it!"

Tears form slightly at the realization that she had just rationalized a reason to return and die on her home planet.

The shocked Commander felt the pull of a reason to land and pushed it away. He looked to see how Kristina was taking this and found a light in her dark smoky eyes. Was it just him or did she look just now like that fierce movie star at the dawn of the digital age who played some woman warrior superhero? The '*Wondrous One*' or something.

"You know, Commander, the private space companies are, were, all employing reusable rockets for automated cargo runs." Kristina added "That would be where gear would be staged for pickup, at the private launch pads. And we have our one shuttle." Elaine loved the idea, sliding over a dozen objections she refused to acknowledge as her mind raced.

Brigham held up his hands in surrender. "All well and good. But unlikely unless those modules up there prove to be for us. First things first." He knew he could not stop them from thinking, but he wanted their full attention on those modules right now. If they did safely land their one shuttle on Earth, it lacked the propulsion to breach Earth's gravity. Refueling? Or could one of the reusable ships travel even if left as ready to go as possible? So many electromechanical devices of man now littered the surface, shorted out or a burnt wreck. Don't think about it now, he admonished himself. Together they went to the bridge with Kristina breaking off for the maintenance shop and then EVA prep.

They must get aboard those ships, she vowed. "We will. Even if I have to thermite my way in."

Coming around the Earth to view Lagrange point 4, they slow the ship to park alongside the collection there. Kristina and Komatsu make the first EVA to the closest one, each carrying a bag of tools they hopefully will not need. The cargo docking port is inspected first.

It seems a perfect match to their own nearly dozen ports. Status lights on the control pad are lit, so a flexible solar array along the cylindrical skin continues to keep batteries at least minimally charged. She and Komatsu give each other a thumbs-up and swing away, using external handholds more than suit jets, to locate a personnel airlock hatch. With relief, the pad here is lit as well and standard design for opening from either direction. The traditional submarine-style wheel would work even in a loss of power. Entering an airlock, a stack of manuals is found within this small space. Realizing the gold they have just found, wrapped in plastic tape labeled 'Demeter', they grab and turn around without entering the module proper. She knows caution and Komatsu readily agrees. These manuals could mean everything.

Sitting together at a common area table under light gravity, packages are slowly, painfully opened one at a time by the Commander. The urge to grab them and start tearing is admirably resisted by all, practically salivating at the possibilities. Brigham tosses each new manual to one crewman at a time; all get several each as he attempts to do at least some kind of modest initial sorting by crew expertise.

'They've had nothing but horror for so long,' he thought but tried not to show it on his face. 'So much pain and grief, the utter failure of our species. Could they still function? Even excel? For that is what is needed now. Can I bring these few examples of humanity back to the excellence of whom they once were?'

'And who brings me back?'

"Ladies and gentlemen, these manuals, this module, and the others, were made for us. They are likely loaded with we know not what, nor what details these manuals contain. Komatsu, you will stay on com, rotating in 12-hour shifts with me. We'll review the executive summaries. We must stay on station here and pray no stray meteor or comet chooses now to cross our path. The rest of you, devour these manuals. We will not board any module until the full scope is understood."

There are almost bursts of dissent, as several want to at least take an initial look, and Jenkins would have tried to dock if he had his way, but discipline held.

"We are a lifeboat. But not for us. For the species. Our seed and eggs can be added to the banks if we work fast." Komatsu and Elaine exchange a glance of hope. She glances at Maha who now has a light in her sultry eyes not seen since before their launch. "But let us not kid ourselves. Judi, how long can we last here without resupply from the surface?"

Having monitored the supply situation with a sharp eye all this time, she knew that critical number. They could do another 7 to 13 months, tops. A low end of 7 with the likely spacewalks required to dock these surprise gifts. If indeed they matched. Surprisingly, with all the current recycling tech there were only a few items needed with which they could last far longer. But not indefinitely. All understood embryos might last in hibernation, but they themselves would not. Hopefully, the module contents out there could change that equation and give them more time, but no matter what they were on a clock.

A finite time. This crew would not live to see a new generation walk the Earth.

As the Commander took in their looks, he wondered about the

other vessels seen floating at other null gravity points, especially the cargo ships at stable L5. Did other nations have their lifeboats out there somewhere, or are they ours as well? Would there soon be several Demeters returning, the same or different than his own, attempting some sort of continuance? Or was this Demeter all there was left of his species?

Judi displayed an introspective look, glancing about at the walls of the great ship.
"Demeter. She was aptly named. The goddess of harvest, growth, and nourishment. She carries the future now. For all of us." Judi searches the faces of the other women for acknowledgment. Maha readily agreed, but openly had eyes now only for the tall Commander, her breath coming slightly heavier, mouth open and moist. He seemed so strong. So dominant. She feels a purpose behind her assignment here more than just the strength of her mind and her degrees.

"Mater omnium nostrum" adds Commander Brigham.

The crew looks at him, surprised anyone but scholars know ancient Latin. He clarifies, "Mother of us all." He sat heavily under the burden of command. The last Commander anywhere. Maha eases onto the bench closely next to him, saying nothing.

Judi nods slowly, "The Demeter AI could be midwife to our species."

Jenkins would have once thought her one of those touchy-feely emotional types before this mission. One of those who see the universe as a living thing. Who see emotional meaning in everything they touch. Belief in sappy poetry to explain existence. Today, he found himself moved by her. The metaphor. Her attempt to put into human words a set of human feelings which did not come with a manual. He needed a manual now. He shocked himself by thinking, "I need the poetry in someone who can make sense of all this!" He shook his head and felt smaller than he had since boyhood. He is not alone in that feeling.

It is Kristina who then takes the floor. Standing with permission of the Commander who has already privately heard what is to come, she launches into the most important mission briefing of her life. Every motivational technique she knows is used. Every inflection and enthusiasm, every demand and plea which turned an enemy informant into an asset, is put to work.

Now is the time, she tells them. Purpose again in the manner of their death. To go out on their feet, not cowering in despondency nor an alcoholic haze. Not for themselves but for what might yet be. They feel hope again in her strong, strident voice. Jenkins is not aware he has risen from his seat as he stares at her impassioned face. She is fiercely alive and all but commands them by her own example to feel the same.

They all entered the sciences, and specifically the space program, for common reasons of the time. Bumper sticker quotes, really. But behind it all, they wished to truly matter. To have a purpose beyond the average human who lived their nearly pointless lives without ever making a difference. How many people were born and lived and died every day for whom the species never took notice? Would never be missed if they had not been born. Would never be remembered. Even genius or kings or queens came and went but the species went on. True meaningful purpose was rare to humans.

She doesn't stop. She doesn't pause. She is merciless to their weaknesses.

This crew would not be remembered. They would never be seen or known by the products of their actions in the little time remaining. These few days and weeks and months. Longer? But they would matter.

Would fight the fight for life within the Demeter until their last breaths. Each swore it to themselves in vows made without words.

***

I can remember this feeling as far back as I remember anything. The muted soft green lighting. The warmth of her on my mouth. The flow. The end of the aching in me that seemed to have no abrupt start and would have no end without her. Her warmth ended the longing. I can remember being cradled often in a soft, warm arm. Head supported. Body supported. Both at once, cradling. Soft and warm. Gently encouraging me towards her softness, her always wet and ready source of my life's strength.

Later, I started ending the ache by various other methods. Methods that do not involve her directly, although I found each new one with her encouragement. Never insisting I use the new source offered, but always letting me know it is there. And always ready to hold and rock me when I feel the need. She is Mother to me. She is my first knowledge of love.

I have noticed that there is more room in my world over time. I remember when there was not much more than Mother's head and arm and the hanging things. Then came things to grasp, which dropped into my world as if out of nowhere, and disappeared as quickly. One day, I determinedly stared right at them for what seemed like forever, to see where they went in the dim time, but I fell asleep. When I woke, they were of course gone again, only to reappear miraculously soon after the light brightened. I tried again, with the same result; having access to them during the bright light time, and them disappearing when the light faded so much one could barely see.

Finally, I tried holding a few of them to me as I rested in the faded light time. I woke with a start when to my surprise they seemed to be slipping out of my arms of their own volition. Amazed, I watched in the dim light as they tumbled and slid towards one side of my world which was colored different than the rest. I grasped two of them, what mother called round-block and square-block, and held them. They seemed to have no will to move anymore. When I put them down, they began sliding again to the same colored section. Again I grasped them and again they stopped, then resumed on being released. I was overjoyed at the new game. Lastly, I let them go and followed them thru the dimness. Sure enough, they went to the same color and – miracle! – the color split open and out of my world they went. Amazing!

I closed my eyes with the deepening dark, smiling and warm with the newfound knowledge, and knowing (hoping?) they would appear yet again tomorrow. It was an especially good night. It always was when I learned something new like that. And the next day, my joy would be rewarded by the world actually growing just a little bit more, and after repeating the new knowledge a few times, more new learning would be offered. More blocks and more complex games. Mother glows in her pleased way. And sings to me.

One day, a scary thing happened. One of the colors not only split open but stayed that way in the bright time. I could see into a distance, the biggest distance I had ever seen in my world, but there seemed to my astonished eyes no clear ending. It was longer than the longest way in my world, a way which was 10 steps if I go on 2 or 20 steps on 4. The newness was so much to look at that I didn't notice at first beyond the smoothness of the opening, round and tightly multicolored like nothing I had ever seen before. Didn't notice that at the far end (there was in fact an end), on one side, the pattern was different.

Bright and clean. No colors. Like most of the edges of my safe warm world.

I kept staring and suddenly realized there was even more to the newness. I jumped aside from the opening, placing my back against the firmness I had known for so long and looking about my world, so safe and warm. I couldn't look into the opening again for some time. Time enough for Mother to prompt me for more feeding. But I was too frightened to do more than crawl to her and let her caress me with her warm, soft arm. I indicated the opening to her without looking at it, but she only held me lightly and stroked my head. Leaving it to me to decide when to pull away from her.

I eventually summoned the courage to look at the opening directly, still in her arm. Then I stood on 2 to see better but still held her with 1. Slowly I approached the opening on 2, glancing back to make sure Mother was still there and hadn't gone asleep. I reached with 1 into the opening and found nothing to stop me. I reached and felt the multicolored sides. They were cold and I jerked back but found nothing different on me. All five littles on the 1 still wiggled and soon were warm again. I touched the side again and found the cold not actually hurtful, but just cool compared to the sides of my own world. Ahead was the corner. There was a place unseen, but somehow I knew it was there.

To see it, I would have to move into the opening myself.

Perhaps it was the knowing that food came and went from openings. Or that the games came and went and returned without damage that gave me the courage to try. Mother simply waited as I took a last look at her, then moved into the opening on 4. After a few steps, I rose to 2, though they shook so much that at first, I thought I would have to go back to 4 again. Moving ahead, I began to see into the far side of the opening.

The concept of around-the-edge became clear, as lo and behold there was another identical opening to the first, another run complete with multicolored sides, and a bright opening at the end. Each of the two ways was easily wide enough for me to move through on either 2 or on 4. No games or hanging things to play with, though. No variation in the colors or texture, still so cool compared to my world.

I realized that if I now continued into the new opening at the end, I would for the first time not see my world. Maybe it wouldn't be there anymore! I ran back to Mother and sat with her for a long while. I ate before the lights began to dim, not from the usual ache but to return to the normalcy I had known. And to make sure that nothing I did had changed anything in my world. Thankfully, the food openings and Mother herself were just the same as when I had left. I rested poorly that dimness, wondering what was beyond. It wasn't until the light came up for the start of a new cycle of brightness that it occurred to me that something could have come thru the opening from the other side. The idea that there was another side was clear to me now. The idea that something might come thru from the other side, just as I had moved partly thru, was an idea that thankfully I did not have during the darkness when Mother was asleep. But thinking on it now, in the bright time, I know that I must go thru. First. I must know, even though it means losing sight of my entire world.

I slowly entered, taking the round-block in one and moving on 2. It gave me something to squeeze. Not as comforting as Mother's arm, but somehow strengthened my resolve to move ahead. I come to the end of the first opening length; I can lean forward and see the second opening extend for an equal distance ahead. After doing that several times, I slip completely around the corner and lose sight of my world.

I stood perfectly still for a few moments, then lean back and glanced around the corner behind me at my world. It is still there, waiting for me. A few repetitions confirmed it. The opening is firm and does not close when I lose sight of it. This is consistent with what happened to the game blocks. I had feared it would be more like the stuff I leaked or dropped, which went into the flowing opening on the floor never to be seen again. No, this was more like the game blocks and the other openings. They would always be there. Brave in my decision, I make my way on 2 down the second run, and as I approached the far opening, I find myself squeezing the round-block so hard I shake a little around it. It is now wet between me and the round block so I shifted it to the other dry little ones and keep moving.

The end of the run looks much like the opening to my world when I glanced back at it. Breathing hard, I lean forward and look around the corner into another whole world!

Easily twice the size of my own, and filled with strange new blocks and wall things, I move into it, spinning as I go, focusing on everything at once and nothing. Several things larger than any game I have ever seen caught my eye, several new small things, all in the familiar colors of the world. Some things move a little when touched, but not on their own. I find that some seem meant to move with just a little encouragement from me.

Others seem to be for playing in one place. What a treasure room! I pick up a few of the small new things, my plain round-block forgotten, and move as fast as 2 can carry me back to my own world. Safe again! So safe I sing out to Mother, who glows into movement and sings with me. I know she is pleased and that I have done a good learning again. We laugh and sing and hold and I show her the new games, though I don't know yet quite what to do with them. The promise of many bright times ahead explodes in my mind. I know joy.

The extension of my world into the new opening happened almost without me realizing it. I knew I could return and must return to my original room to ease the aching for food, have a place to rest in the dim hours near Mother, and get rid of the stuff I leak before it begins to smell and mess up the games. Mother never likes that (and neither do I). I prefer to do all my eating and cleaning myself now, although now and then Mother offers me a small something and says its good for me. She is Mother and I always take it/them gladly.

The new part of my world begins to challenge me with changing shapes on several sections of one wall. I learn to manipulate the images with knobs and keys and things to touch which are connected to the wall shape screens with long, soft things, thinner than my smallest finger, but as long as my longest arm.

Instead of singing, like Mother, the wall screens make noises with the images and I begin to learn their way. It grows somewhat boring at first, but the first time I mastered something new, it lit up with one of Mother's favorite reward songs. I was rewarded further, with images of one of the physical games and how it moved or worked.

This was great. I could learn all kinds of things like this.

One of the first things I've learned was that each different thing has a sound, while many of the same kind of thing has a different sound. I already knew this concept, but did not know I knew it because of the smallness of my old room and the small number of things in it. I really like this concept, and Mother repeats the new names for things I tell her I saw today, the tone is always a little different than mine, but we have always understood each other quite well. And Mother calls me Charlie. And I call out Mother to her. It seems always to have been like that, but I can't quite remember. Things in my big world grow a lot more complicated than naming the few things back in my small world. But the idea is the same, and Mother is always so pleased when I learn. And this part of the world, too, grows larger a little with each new big learning. Only the connecting run seems to remain the same in size.

They were good times. Time passed and kept passing. The only other time I've been really scared was when a new screen appeared near the teaching ones. This had no controls or buttons but simply reflected my face. It was wondrous looking at others on the teaching screens, though a little confusing at first. But they were just flat things on the screens and never reached into my world until the holos started. Even then, they were just images and sound.

This was different.

The image I saw moved when I moved, turned, and went away as I did, and was essentially another me. That took some getting used to, but when I told Mother about it, Mother showed me another one with both of us in it. It became clear that it was only an image of what was right in front of it. I even found I could take the small one from Mother's room and use it to look around the corner down the hall or into the room ahead without exposing me! Neat!

Time has passed some more. I find the screens good to learn how to use the new games and devices, but once learned I'd rather just get good with the devices themselves by directly playing with each and forget the screens. The devices for running and pushing let me feel good afterward when I sometimes feel like running between the rooms but just move too fast now for that distance, once seeming so large, to satisfy the need. Mother is still there to hug me and explain things the screen didn't make clear, but it's also clear now that the screens have taught me things even Mother doesn't know or understand. And I can't remember the last time I went to Mother when the hungry ache comes. I feel myself in growth.

The AOE-SIM game on the screen is the only one that I still like from when I was small. When I still moved on 4 occasionally. It is challenging to have some of the villagers cut wood while others dig for metal or stone, others pick berries or plant a farm. You have to keep an eye on them, though, because after a while the farms don't grow unless you replant and the lumberjacks don't know where to look for new wood unless I scroll around and find some for them.

The scouts are really neat, cause they move so much faster than the villagers and see so much farther on the horse that always moves on 4, but you have to watch out for wolves and the bad villagers who don't plant or build, but just come now and then to take what you have or hurt your villagers. I started losing interest for a while until I found another village like the one I controlled which planted and built as my people did. We started trading and things got more interesting for a while. Some villagers even started suggesting new types of buildings or techniques or devices to build.

Just in time it seemed, every time things started getting too easy.

The plow and the double bit ax were really good ideas and increased production a lot. Which you needed for famine or stormy times. Else everyone would die and I had to start over, again and again. Things like rotating crops and using the goat and rabbit droppings to bring back old farmland. Like terracing acreage and smelting metal out of certain rocks. The wheel and the fishing pole, the net and bow.

Tomorrow Mother says will be the last day alone for me. I have never felt alone, since Mother is always there for me, and the screen teachers talk to me and respond, though without seeming to really see me as Mother does. She says there is a lot more, that I will understand when I see other worlds than the one I have known. Other worlds, just as there are more than one screen teacher, more than one villager in my village, and more than one room in my world. I asked Mother if there were more than one Mother and me. I never understood the meaning of her replies until now, when she repeats I won't be alone anymore.

It's kind of scary. Others who may play games and control villagers onscreen and run and climb and do things and figure things out, but different than me. Not in my control. Not raised by my Mother. What if their Mothers are different? What will they be like without a wonderful, warm Mother like mine? Do they even have Mothers? All these things remain unanswered. Mother won't say more, that I must explore for myself. She reminds me of my exploring the two rooms of my world and how exciting that was. Exploring the worlds on the screen too, of 3D oceans and land and mountains and rivers. I've mastered all kinds of skills and my body is strong and fast, but will that be enough? Do I actually know anything worth knowing?

Today is the day. I wake, as usual, work out and eat a little breakfast as usual, and check the screen in the big room for today's instructions. But there is none. No list of tasks or skills to master. It simply says/writes I'm 2400 days old, 2400 light/dark cycles. And there is nothing more for them to teach me here. I am to take the portable screen and go to the panel. I touch the proper combination of colored buttons and speak the single password - "EARTH". The panel falls away and reveals yet another room.

I expected this, but not the size.

The ceiling is what I know is called vaulted, but seeing it is nothing like seeing only screen images and holograms I know are not real. Not physical like this. It takes my breath away. The far side of the enclosure is so far away that another opening like the one I'm passing through is half size in my vision. Yet I know it is not a mirror or screen image.

I know because there is another in the opening, and it's not me or a mirror of me. It's a little different.

There are other openings as well, 2 meters apart, so that six, no, seven openings including mine, make up the circular enclosure. But only three others are open and have someone peering out.

Two of them do look a lot like me, but the third has much longer hair streaming from his head. And no penis. This must be the female type. The males regard him curiously, and he shifts and blushes the way I know I have when Mother catches me doing something dumb that I had already mastered previously. But he doesn't run away. Just stares out at us bravely, each in turn. He then walks out into the middle of the enclosure, portable screen in both hands, whereas we three carry ours in one.

We approach him, and he smiles. We three smile in turn, and now it is we who are blushing. Clearly possessing knowledge beyond ours. He puts his portable down and takes one of our hands in each of his. The feel is soft and warm like Mother, but different. Harder and softer at the same time. Good. Somehow good. He smells good too. I exchange names with Eric, Peter, and JeanKathryn.

Still holding hands, we look up at the big screen overhead in the pod and hear a final lesson. The lesson of departure. Of pods dropping from orbit down to the surface. Of starting a village in physical space. Each is assigned tasks, for well known are our individual strengths, but the vault teacher leaves it to us to divide the nonessential tasks. This Teacher knows each of us and has complete confidence that we can start the village together, with a mobile Mother to help us.

Another mobile Mother has already podded down and has prepared for us. It is a bit frightening and we are all four nearly tearful, knowing we will no longer return to our original Mothers. But want the new adventure and are comforted that a Mother of sorts will be with us. Others will follow us. But we are the first. We are told but do not understand fully that we will be the elders of our people, and will in time take back our huge homeworld. A world cleansed by time. Cleansed by blowing winds, by falling rains, by the natural decay of harmful agents.

We understand breeding will one day be required. It appears to be a comical thing, though the seriousness of it is clear to us. Each successful pairing with a female will produce another villager within 300 days; each new villager can begin to work after 2000 days and reproduce in turn after 6000 days, so we have time yet. The light and dark cycles are grouped into 365.23 = 1 annum. Every thirty days we will see the other light in the sky at its fullest, our world's one moon. Vault teacher says every annum the Mothers will send us from 1 to 7 new villagers, aged as we are today. We each do the math quickly in our minds without needing the portables. These will grow the village to approx 30-50 in nine more annum, all sent and not including any grown ourselves. Thereafter, the breeding of each female will start to contribute to the total.

Not counting losses from wolves or other death, ten more annum beyond that will see us at 80 bred + 30 more sent + original 30 = 140. The screens have taught us that 70 is a genetically self-sustaining population, as long as we cull the young, so even when that terrible day comes that all the robotic Mothers here in orbit fail, as we are told two already have, there shall be enough of us to go on. To succeed.

"Two Mothers failed?" JeanKathryn asks in a sad but strong voice, asking what we are all thinking "but there are only four of us here from seven little room-worlds, and two Mothers failed, so what happened to the others? The others like us?" The reply is a description of culling the young to keep the herd strong. We males shudder but the female seems to grasp the need quicker and the certain truth of it.

Still holding hands, we are led by what appears to be a Mother, a new type to us, for she moves as we do on 2. This Mother leads us to an entrance to what the vaulted teacher calls a pod. Rounded on the inside, and bubbled with small round appendages on the outside, it is soft and flexible but has immense strength to it. The entrance is big enough for each of us to pass thru. Inside, we see the sides have recessed enclosures for seven of us, and a docking station for the mobile Mother. The center of the interior is almost completely occupied by lashed devices and equipment.

We reluctantly part hands and take our places in the recessed alcoves. We have to slide carefully around the centered gear, placing our portables in the slots made for them. A pair of stacked wheel barrels are anchored at the center. They are filled with containers which themselves look useful, but are no doubt also filled with devices and seeds for us. Hammers and assorted nails, numerous carving tools, an anvil, and pairs of hoes, axes, and shovels with plastic handles. Several bows and quivers of arrows. Many other tools and blades without handles, but that's ok since we each have seen the videos on carving. The Mother says the seed containers can be resealed and used to store food and water. The Mother comes and goes, bringing a little extra equipment to fill the unused alcoves. So odd to see a mobile Mother. Banana tree seeds, asparagus, and various nuts not part of what she calls the 'core supplies'. She assures us that mass balance is maintained, though the landing will be quite bumpy for minutes on end - by design. She moves out of the doorway and straps in as well. It seals, so smoothly we can hardly see the joining.

And perhaps one day a scout of ours will find another village, starting from any other surviving lifeboat in orbit. There were precious few lifeboats intended. There may have been only this one, or just this one remaining. Contact by the ship AI to anything else was lost in the long wait. Waiting all these decades for the air below to clear. For the contaminated flora and fauna to wash away. Waiting for the sensors to say it is alright to start incubating the frozen embryos. To send them armed with plant seeds and pre-industrial age skills and portable screens of stored knowledge. Up to steam and Newton.

To begin again, before the aged solar cells have too many losses to power this ship, still maintaining its L4 post, having survived meteors and solar radiations and mechanical failures. To begin again before the frozen embryos refuse to thaw. Before those who do thaw are too defective to be allowed to reach their 2400th day. Robotic Mothers onboard will again and again cull their young, just as they have taught the females to do once on planet. Four out of seven for a first orbital crop. Just another 9 annum of annual drops and then seed-ship will try again with another village, perhaps close by at a slow river beneath the mountains. And then another beyond that. For as long as the power and embryos and Mothers hold out. For as long as the will of man lives on in his technology, and fights the fight for life, even beyond the death of man himself on what once was long ago and is now again the sweet Earth.

***

ABOUT THE AUTHOR

Charlie Marino was born in the Bronx, New York and holds a BS and MS in nuclear engineering from Columbia University. His various occupations included bond and commodities trading, founding several small computer companies, and now writes sci-fi novels and short stories. He has more robots than friends, but they're good ones. The author makes his home in the mountains of America, where he helps the nice folks at SETI & carves his own wooden chess sets.

These short stories followed his debut novel, 'Dominant Life Form', available online as e-book, paperback, or hardcover in a dozen countries. Look for additional full novels being published soon!

If you enjoyed these stories, please consider leaving a positive review at your favorite retailer. Or contact me on social media with your suggestions!
Thanks! - your humble scribbler

Printed in Great Britain
by Amazon